TAKE A
WALK WITH
ME

MARCIA LYNN McCLURE

Published by Distractions Ink
P.O. Box 15971
Rio Rancho, NM 87174

Published by Distractions Ink
©Copyright 2011 by M. Meyers
A.K.A. Marcia Lynn McClure
Cover Photography by
©Hlphoto | Dreamstime.com
Cover Design by
Sheri L. Brady | MightyPhoenixDesignStudio.com

First Printed Edition: August 2011

McClure, Marcia Lynn, 1965—
Take a Walk with Me: a novella/by Marcia Lynn McClure.

ISBN: 978-0-9838074-6-9

Library of Congress Control Number: 2011936836

Printed in the United States of America

To Weezy, Danielle, Lisa, June, and Stacey—
Barnes & Noble never was so fun.
Thanks for the laughter, love, and friendship!
"T.D. and W."

CHAPTER ONE

Cozy Robbins exhaled a long sigh. She was tired, and her eyelids felt droopy. Yawning, she leaned back in her chair, running her fingers up through her long hair and stretching her arms over her head. Glancing to the clock on the wall, Cozy wondered how she had managed to finish thirty more Christmas tree ornaments before midnight. Of course, these were only tiny clay mice tucked snuggly beneath hand-stitched quilts in walnut shell cradles. They weren't as tedious to make as the hinged walnut halves with Christmas tree and fireplace scenes depicted inside them. Still, they were far more difficult to craft than the simple gold-paint-dipped walnuts with ribbon loops Cozy also made.

She shook her head, wondering how in the world she had gotten herself into taking so many orders again. Things certainly had escalated in the past five years. It seemed difficult to fathom—the hundreds of ornament orders she still needed to fill—when just five years previous, she'd been astonished at having sold sixty ornaments total.

Cozy closed her eyes and sighed once more in

thinking back to the November she had been sixteen—to the first series of finely crafted walnut ornaments she'd made to sell. She'd wanted to purchase something nice for her Grandma Robbins for Christmas that year—a beautiful set of bookends she'd seen in a specialty shop, knights in armor posed in kissing princesses. The moment she'd seen the bookends, she'd known they were just what her grandmother had been looking for to adorn the bookshelf in her entryway. But they were costly, priced at nearly three hundred dollars for the set.

At sixteen, three hundred dollars was hard to come by, especially when it was to be spent on only one gift. Still, the bookends were ideal for her grandmother, and Cozy had begun to ponder ways she could make the three hundred dollars—for in truth, how often did the perfect Christmas gift present itself? Ironically, it had been her Grandma Robbins who had suggested Cozy make and sell her charming walnut Christmas tree ornaments. Though she had no idea why Cozy wanted to acquire three hundred dollars, Dottie Robbins (the very person for whom Cozy was inspired to earn the money) suggested her granddaughter sell the delicately crafted Christmas ornaments.

Cozy's grandmother had always adored Cozy's walnut ornaments. In fact, Cozy had begun making them for her grandmother in the first place. She'd been ten years old and wanting to give her grandma something special. She had seen a plastic walnut ornament in a bin at a second-hand store. The plastic half walnut shell had a little plastic mouse nestled in it, nibbling on a piece of cheese and wearing a Santa hat. Cozy thought it was the most adorable thing she had ever seen and begged her mother for fifty cents to purchase it. The little Christmas tree ornament had fast become Cozy's greatest treasure. To some, it may not have been worth even the fifty cents, but to Cozy it was priceless.

Consequently, Cozy had spent an entire afternoon cracking open walnuts and hollowing out the insides until she found just the perfect shells to make her own ornaments. She used gray molding clay to form little mouse heads. Carefully she'd painted tiny black eyes and noses and nestled them into the shells. With old fabric scraps her mother had given her, she then cut and stitched tiny quilt tops, tucking them snugly around the little clay mice. She had figured out how to fashion a way to hang the ornaments by using lengths of gold thread so that the walnut cradle would hang perfectly from any Christmas tree branch.

Cozy had presented these first walnut ornaments to her grandmother on Christmas Eve that year. Dottie Robbins had been delighted to literal tears, claiming Cozy's walnut cradle ornaments were the most wonderful gift she'd ever received. After that Christmas, Cozy worked on improving her ornaments. Every year she presented her grandma with several new walnut ornaments, and Dottie was always just as excited as she had been the day she received the first ones. Gradually, Cozy began to diversify her craft. She hollowed out walnuts by the hundreds. Some she would glue back together, painting them gold and adding a red ribbon at the top to provide a means of hanging it. Her favorite ornaments, however, were the ones with two walnut halves hinged together. When opened, they revealed either a miniature nativity scene or a miniature Christmas scene—one half having a tiny Christmas tree with gifts at its base nestled within and the other boasting a little fireplace, complete with stockings hanging from the mantel. These required a lot more work with clay and detailed painting, but they were Cozy's favorites. Yes, her walnut ornaments had become quite popular around town.

As Cozy tucked one special ornament into a small white box with her gold embossed logo (two robins sitting on a holly branch, their heads lovingly pressed together and the trade name *Cozy Robbins* beneath them) stamped on the top, she wished she could see the look on the girl's face when her boyfriend handed her the ornament and told her to open it. The young man had contacted Cozy about a making a specialty ornament. She had agreed to do it, of course—to hide the diamond solitaire engagement ring inside a gold, red-velvet-lined walnut.

"How romantic!" she sighed, smiling and setting the box aside. She glanced at the clock again, even though she already knew the time. She had to get to bed. Her shift started early, and she didn't want to be too tired.

Exhaling another sigh of weariness, Cozy rose from her chair. Two more semesters and she'd have her degree. Surely she could stop waiting tables at the café then. She glanced at the table covered with Christmas ornaments made from walnuts. She could hardly believe she'd managed to pay for every one of her winter college semesters with the proceeds from selling such a little thing. Oh, it was a ton of work—no doubt it was. Still, the whole concept that walnuts could pay for a college education was almost unfathomable.

Reaching over to the electrical outlet nearby, Cozy unplugged the Christmas lights she'd strewn over the ceiling of the basement. She blew out the pumpkin-spice-scented candle on the table and turned off the old stereo, and the soothing music she listened to while working at night was silenced. The basement room that had seemed so warm and inviting a moment before was dark and cold and quiet now. Cozy smiled, amazed at what a few Christmas lights, an aromatic fragrance, and some soothing music could do to brighten up a dark space.

Hurrying up the stairs, Cozy brushed her teeth, threw on a pair of pajamas, and fell into bed. Morning and the early birds who frequented the café would arrive all too soon. Still, Cozy smiled, for a vision of her grandmother's delight at seeing the new ornaments Cozy had made for her lingered in her mind like a comforting dream. Grandma Dottie always brightened Cozy's day. Therefore, Cozy decided to look on waitressing at the café the next morning as a means to a happy end. She hadn't seen her grandma in almost a week and could hardly wait to leave work and drive over to see her the next day.

She loved spending time with her Grandma Robbins—she always had. As far back as Cozy could remember, her grandmother had been one of the most wonderful things in the world to her. Cozy knew Dottie Robbins's affection, influence, and love had helped shape her life—still did shape it—and she could not imagine an existence without her.

With one final sigh, Cozy's mind wandered toward sleep with the tender memory of being two or three years old and her grandmother pushing her in the old swing that still hung, faded and worn, from one T-bar under the clothesline in Dottie Robbins's backyard. In her mind, she could still hear her grandma singing "The Teddy Bears' Picnic" as she gently pushed the swing and then attached a sheet to the clothesline with a clothespin from her apron pocket. Cozy could almost feel the warm breeze on her face as it billowed the clean white sheets hanging on the line—still hear the birds as they twittered around her grandmother's bird feeder— still smell the sweet perfume of freshly mown grass...

❦

"Cozy!"

Cozy turned to see Mindy hurrying after her.

"Have you got any extra ornaments?" Mindy asked, rushing toward Cozy's car. "I know I already put my order in, but I forgot a couple of people."

Though the question rather deflated her enthusiasm, Cozy smiled at her friend. A sale was a sale and meant more money for tuition—whether or not she was getting tired of walnuts. She felt a giggle tickle her throat as Mindy characteristically puffed at the blond bangs on her forehead.

"Sure," Cozy answered with more enthusiasm than she really felt. "How many were you wanting? I'm still making them right now...so if there's something special you want..."

"I want four nestled mice cradle ones and four hinged nativities, if it doesn't stress you out too much," Mindy answered. Again she puffed at her bangs. Cozy felt her heart lighten even for having to make eight more last-minute ornaments. Mindy was too sweet—too kind and supportive of Cozy as a friend and a customer—for Cozy to deny her anything.

"Eight? That's a couple?" Cozy asked.

Mindy shrugged. "I guess it's more like a few, right?"

"I guess," Cozy giggled.

"Do you mind?" Mindy ventured. "I know you like to have the orders before now."

"I don't mind at all," Cozy answered with a just little less than perfect honesty. "Are you sure you want to spend that much though? That's eighty bucks...I mean, forty."

"I'm sure," Mindy confirmed. "Can I bring some cash tomorrow?"

"Yeah...but why don't you just make it twenty."

"Cozy Robbins," Mindy scolded. "You have got to quit underselling your stuff! Your ornaments are so charming, and they're hard to make, I'm sure. Ten dollars apiece is a steal, and you should quit cutting your friends and family that crazy five-dollar discount on each one. I'm paying eighty."

"No," Cozy argued. She hated charging her friends and family anything at all, and she certainly wasn't going to let them pay full price. "I'll take twenty…or I won't make them for you."

"Cozy," Mindy scolded.

Cozy sighed, relenting, "Okay then. Forty. Dang! That's like four movies at the theatre…or a new pair of shoes…or—"

"Stop it!" Mindy giggled. "They're worth it, Cozy. They are the most adorable things in the world! People are willing to pay for adorable…so let them. Okay?"

"Okay." Cozy shook her head, still unable to believe someone would drop even a dime on Christmas ornaments made out of walnuts. Her smile for Mindy broadened—for if there was one thing her ornament sales had taught her, it was who her true friends were. So many people asked for freebies because they knew Cozy personally. Yet she found that her real friends understood she made the ornaments as a supplement to her income. Her genuine friends never tried to take advantage of her or haggle her down. It was a valuable life lesson to her—and an example she followed in her own dealings with friends. Still, she absolutely loathed letting them pay for anything. But she knew it was important to Mindy that she take some kind of remuneration.

"Good. I'll bring cash tomorrow," Mindy said, smiling.

"If you must…but it's still a waste of forty bucks," Cozy giggled.

"Shut up!" Mindy laughed. "I have to get back… so have fun with your grandma. I know she'll love the new ornaments."

"Thanks," Cozy said. Nodding toward the café, she added, "And good luck tonight."

Mindy's eyebrows arched with understanding. "Thanks. I hate the dinner shift."

"Sorry."

Mindy shrugged. "I'm fine. Just thankful to have the job, you know?"

"I do know," Cozy agreed.

"Okay then…have fun."

"You too."

Cozy watched Mindy return to the café, silently reminded herself how glad she was not to have the dinner shift, and felt guilty.

Opening her car door, Cozy turned when she heard a familiar rustle. The leaves of the cottonwoods were quickly changing from green to gold as autumn descended in its full beauty. She paused a moment, for she had promised herself a long time before that she would always, always take the time to watch the leaves transform in the fall—that she would never, never be too busy with ornaments or work or anything else to miss it.

She lingered in watching the breath of the breeze

cause the green and yellow leaves to tremble. The air was crisp and refreshing. The moment soothed Cozy even more than punching out from work had, and she felt her smile broaden.

She got into her car, turned the key in the ignition, and pulled out of the café parking lot. She hoped her grandmother had planned meatloaf and mashed potatoes for supper; she loved her grandma's meatloaf and mashed potatoes. In fact, it was the only meatloaf she really liked. There was something special about her grandma's meatloaf—something nostalgic and old-fashioned—and Cozy's mouth began to water as she drove toward the bridge.

"Over the river and through the cottonwoods," she said aloud to herself. With a delighted giggle of anticipation, she began to hum the familiar words to the song that had prompted her thoughts. Secretly, she loved the fact she had to drive over the river and through the cottonwoods to get to her grandmother's house. Cozy thought of the way her mother used to sing the song every time the family traveled to her grandmother's house when she was a child. It was a wonderful little sentiment—a wonderful memory—and it added another measure of joy to her already happy mood.

❦

"Grandma? I'm here," Cozy called as she closed the front door behind her. "Grandma?"

"In here, sweet pea!" Dottie Robbins called from the other room.

Cozy smiled. Her grandmother's voice was like music. How she loved the happy sound of it.

Setting a basket of new walnut ornaments on the entryway table, Cozy hurried toward the kitchen. She could already smell the meatloaf cooking. Supper would be delicious—as was always the case at her grandma's house.

"Hi, Grandma," Cozy said as she entered the kitchen to see her grandmother peering out through one of the windows.

"My angel!" Dottie said, turning from the window and drawing Cozy into a warm embrace. Cozy smiled as the light fragrance of rose perfume tickled her nostrils. "It seems a coon's age since you've been here."

"I know," Cozy agreed. "I'm sorry. I've just been so busy that I—"

"I know, sweet pea," Dottie said. "But you're here now, and we're going to have a wonderful evening!"

"As always," Cozy said as her grandma released her.

"I've got a meatloaf in the oven, and…" Dottie began, clasping her hands together just like an excited child, "and I'm hoping you brought me some new ornaments today."

"I certainly did." She frowned as uncertainty washed over her. "I hope you like them this year. I did a few things differently and—"

"I'll love them, and you know it!" Dottie laughed.

Cozy studied her grandmother for a moment—her smiling, twinkling blue eyes, the sweet little wrinkles on her face. Her grandmother's hair had once been a dark,

dark chocolate-brown like Cozy's, but it had faded to a beautiful snowy white. Cozy thought it was very becoming and hoped her hair would do the same—but not until she was in her sixties like her grandmother was.

Dottie Robbins glanced to the window she'd been gazing through when Cozy had entered the room. Cozy frowned, curious—wondering what could be so interesting.

"What are you looking at, Grandma?" Cozy asked, going to the window.

"The handsomest hunk of burning love I've seen in a long, long time…that's what," Dottie sighed.

"What?" Cozy giggled. She looked out the window to see an elderly man raking leaves in the backyard next door. "Who's that?" she asked.

"My new hunk of burning love neighbor, that's who," Dottie answered.

"Grandma!" Cozy exclaimed. She laughed. Her grandma was so funny sometimes.

"Well, just look at him!" Dottie said, nodding toward the window. "Isn't he just the dreamiest man ever?"

Cozy gazed out the window once more, giggling as she studied the man. He was tall, silver-haired, and as tan as leather. He wore an old barn jacket and worn-out work boots, and Cozy shrugged, thinking he was indeed a striking figure. She couldn't see his face very clearly, but it was obvious he was a hard worker.

"He moved in last week," Dottie offered, "and I've

been watching out my windows every day since. He's got the deepest blue eyes. They just set my heart to palpitating!"

"Grandma…you have a crush?" Cozy teased.

Dottie smiled. "Of course, angel! Wouldn't you if you were my age?"

Cozy's smile faded just a little. When her Grandpa Robbins had passed away seven years before, the family feared Dottie might follow him too soon. A deep, aching depression and loneliness had overtaken her grandmother. It was one reason Cozy had begun to visit her at least once a week—to remind Dottie Robbins how loved she was and to cheer her up. It had taken a couple of years for Dottie to return to some semblance of the woman she'd been before her husband's death. Therefore, it was surprising to see her puppy-eyed over another man.

Even so, Cozy felt her heart leap a little. It was wonderful to see her grandmother so rosy-cheeked and excited. She thought for a moment that her grandma looked like a schoolgirl in that moment, blushing with the excitement of a new boy in the neighborhood.

"Well? What's his name?" she asked her grandmother.

Dottie's smile broadened. "Buckly Bryant…Buck for short," she answered. "Isn't that a wonderful name? It sounds like he just rode into town on a white horse, doesn't it?"

"Yeah, it does," Cozy agreed. "So you've met him then?"

"Of course! I went over and introduced myself last Thursday while the movers were moving his things in. I swear, Cozy…he put my heart to hammering like a woodpecker!"

Cozy giggled as her grandma placed a hand over her heart as if it were still hammering. "Well, good! You need a little romance and excitement in your life, Grandma."

"Do I?"

Cozy nodded, noting the pink that rose to her grandma's cheeks. "Of course! Everyone needs it…and you deserve it too."

Dottie glanced out the window once more—rather longingly—and exhaled a wistful sigh. "He is a tall drink of water, isn't he?"

"Yes, he is," Cozy agreed.

With one final sigh, Dottie turned her attention from the window and her handsome neighbor in his backyard to Cozy. "Well, as I said…I've got the meatloaf in the oven. We can put the potatoes on in about an hour. Meanwhile…" She paused, gleeful anticipation twinkling in her blue eyes. "Meanwhile, show me what you've made this year. I've been so excited to see the new ornaments! I could hardly wait. I almost snuck down to the basement last time I was at your house… but your father stopped me."

Cozy laughed. "Oh, Dad's very protective about my ornaments," she explained. "He doesn't want the surprise ruined for anyone. Still, it's not like they're really any different than the ones I've made in the past."

"Cosette Robbins!" Dottie scolded. "That is simply not true. Why...every year they're different. And I don't know how you manage it...but they keep getting better and better."

"You're my grandma. You have to say that," Cozy said.

"I am your grandma...but I'm sincere in my compliments."

Cozy nodded. "Okay then, come and see what you think."

Dottie rubbed her hands together like a silent-movie villain as Cozy went to the entryway and retrieved the basket of ornaments she'd brought. Returning to the kitchen, she set the basket in the center of the table.

"Oh, I can hardly stand it. The anticipation is glorious!" Dottie exclaimed, sitting down in a chair and pulling the basket to her.

Cozy sat down next to her and tried to hide her amusement in her grandma's delight. She bit her lip, unable to hide her relief and pleasure as her grandma gasped when she opened the first little white box.

"Oh, Cozy. It's adorable! Simply too adorable for words," Dottie exclaimed as she carefully took the small walnut cradle, complete with a mouse reading a tiny copy of "The Night Before Christmas" and tucked beneath a red flannel quilt. A miniature oil lamp on one edge of the walnut cradle and a tiny green nightcap for the mouse completed the scene.

Again Dottie gasped with awe. "I *love* it, Cozy. Oh, I love it!" She picked up her reading glasses from the old lazy Susan that had lived in the center of her kitchen table for as long as Cozy could remember. "Oh, look at that! How did you ever paint the title on that book? And look at the little lamp. Oh, Cozy…I *love* it! I just *love* it. Just look at the stitching on the quilt! Oh, however do you manage to make the stitches so small? Oh, I love it. I absolutely love it!"

Cozy smiled. She could tell when her grandma was sincere in her compliments, and she was certainly sincere. She felt relieved—and elated.

"Well, if you like that one, then you should freak out over this one," Cozy said, taking another box from the basket and handing it to her grandmother.

Dottie paused and inspected the *Cozy Robbins* logo embossed on the box's lid. "I have to admit, I'm kind of proud of myself for thinking of this—the two little birds…the two cozy robins."

Dottie giggled, and Cozy said, "You should be. It was very clever."

"And memorable," Dottie added. "People remember it. Something this cute sticks in their minds."

"I know…and I'm glad."

Dottie reached out, cupping Cozy's cheek with one hand. "I love you, sweet pea," she said.

"I love you too, Grandma," Cozy said, taking her grandma's hand in her own and squeezing it for a moment. "Now…see if you like the others."

"Oh, I know I will, sweetheart. I know I will."

Cozy sighed. She loved her grandmother so much! What would she ever do without her?

❦

"So? Where did he move from?" Cozy asked, dipping a forkful of mashed potatoes into the melted butter puddle at the center of the far too large helping of mashed potatoes her grandmother had plopped on her plate.

"The east side," Dottie answered. "He said he'd always wanted to live in the valley, along the river. So when the opportunity presented itself, he moved. He lost his wife a few years ago and was having trouble with the blues, as he put it. He's a retired firefighter."

"Wow! A real-life hero, huh?" Cozy asked, smiling.

"Well, he sure looks the part!" Dottie giggled. "I swear, Cozy...I had butterflies in my stomach the whole time he was talking to me! For a minute there, I felt like I was seventeen and he was the proverbial captain of the football team, you know?"

"I can imagine," Cozy said. She smiled as she took a bite of meatloaf.

"What?" Dottie asked.

Cozy shrugged. "Nothing. I was just thinking."

"Thinking what? I know that look. You're up to mischief, Cozy."

Cozy sighed. "I was just thinking that maybe Mr. Buckly Bryant will whisk you away on some romantic adventure. He looks like he's a good kisser."

"Oh, for pity's sake, Cozy!" Dottie laughed. "The things you come up with. What an outlandish thing to say!"

But Cozy saw the merry twinkle in her

grandmother's blue eyes. She wished for a moment that her own eyes were blue. Cozy had her father's hazel eyes, but she'd always wished they'd been blue. Still, she contented herself with being glad she had her grandmother's chocolate hair.

"It's not outlandish," Cozy argued. "He's a hunk of burning love. You said so yourself. And you're ravishing. You'd make a perfect couple."

"Now stop that teasing, Cozy Robbins," Dottie playfully scolded. "You're being ridiculous, and you know it."

"No, I'm not, Grandma," Cozy argued. She paused a moment and then suggested, "You should bake him some of your banana nut bread and take it over—you know, as a housewarming, welcome-to-the-neighborhood sort of thing. Once he tastes your banana nut bread, you'll have him eating out of the palm of your hand."

Dottie smiled and laughed a little. "You know, maybe I should." She shrugged. "I mean, it *would* be the neighborly thing to do."

"It would be," Cozy encouraged. "And I still say he looks like a good kisser!"

"Cozy Robbins!" Dottie scolded. "Shame on you."

Still, Cozy could tell by the blush rising to her grandma's cheeks that she was thinking the same thing.

"Grandma...I love your meatloaf and mashed potatoes," Cozy sighed.

"Thank you, darling." Dottie placed a warm palm to Cozy's cheek. Nodding to the small blue bowl of green beans on the table, she added, "And those are the last of the green beans from my garden for this year."

"They're delicious," Cozy assured her.

"I know," Dottie said, shrugging her shoulder with delighted pride.

Cozy laughed. She felt as if she were caught in a moment of perfect wonder. Sitting at her grandmother's table enjoying a supper of meatloaf, mashed potatoes, and green beans—it was peaceful, warm, comfortable, and relaxing. The rhythmic ticking of the clock on the wall was soothing, and Cozy sighed. It was a moment to cherish, as was every moment spent with her grandmother, and Cozy consciously committed it to memory.

"I suppose women my age do still kiss, don't they?" Dottie asked.

"Of course they do, Grandma," Cozy exclaimed. "If Grandpa were still here…wouldn't you still be kissing him?"

Dottie smiled a melancholy smile and whispered, "Yes. Definitely yes."

Cozy's heart ached, knowing she may have caused her grandmother pain in provoking a memory of loss. "I'm sorry, Grandma. I only meant—"

"I know, darling," Dottie soothed, smiling. "And you're right." Her smile broadened. "Mr. Buckly Bryant does look like a good kisser."

Cozy giggled and took another bite of butter-slathered mashed potatoes. The cuckoo clock in the hallway announced six o'clock, and Cozy was glad the time was ticking by slowly. There would always be ornaments to make, bills to pay, and things to do, but there wouldn't always be time with her grandma. At least she had that priority straight.

"So are you dating anyone yet, honey?" Dottie asked.

Cozy sighed. "I went out with Tristan Plummer last Friday."

"And how did that go?"

Cozy shrugged. "Okay, I guess. But he's so...so..."

"Soft?" Dottie suggested.

"Exactly!" Cozy confirmed. "Like I might expect to see him coming out of the nail salon with a new manicure or something. His hands are so...you know..."

"Soft," Dottie reiterated.

Cozy nodded. "Yeah."

Dottie sighed. "I worry for you girls today, sweet pea. Masculinity itself is under attack, it seems. Society is forcing men from their natural, instinctive path. Men weren't made to be cooped up in a cubicle unable to do anything physical. They were made to be hunter-gatherers, to work hard in body and mind. It's hard for men these days...for women too. Femininity isn't what it used to be either."

Cozy sighed, for she agreed—wholeheartedly. Yet what could be done about it? Society was what it was, and it certainly wasn't going to let up.

"Well, Mr. Buckly Bryant looks masculine enough," Cozy offered.

"Yes, he does," Dottie whispered with a wink.

"You definitely need to whip up a batch of your banana nut bread, Grandma," Cozy giggled.

"I think you might be right, sweet pea."

"Of course I'm right," Cozy said, dipping another forkful of mashed potatoes into the butter well on her plate.

❦

Later that night, Cozy sat in her bed, writing in her journal while tucked comfortably beneath a soft flannel quilt. She had had a productive day and a tranquil, wonderful evening with her grandmother. She was tired but truly content.

Still, it seemed contentment never lasted long. Cozy's bedroom door suddenly burst open, and the peaceful moment was shattered as her younger sister Ashley literally hopped into the room.

"Can I borrow your pink sweater for tomorrow, Cozy?" Ashley asked.

Cozy sighed, wishing she could have afforded to live on campus for one more semester at least. The lack of privacy in living at home was so frustrating sometimes. Still, she loved her home—and her family—even if her little brothers and sisters did drive her nuts.

"I guess so, Ash," Cozy answered.

Ashley smiled and hurried to Cozy's closet.

"Why are you in bed so early?" Ashley asked. "It's only ten."

"Why are you up so late? It's already ten," Cozy teased.

Ashley smiled. "I'm totally nervous, that's why! I don't think I'm gonna sleep a wink tonight!"

"Why's that?" Cozy asked—even though she already suspected there was boy at the core of Ashley's discontent.

"Because Kaylee *swears* she heard Braden Lewis telling a friend that Dylan Hill is going to ask me to the winter formal tomorrow night. And if you want to know the truth...I'm totally freaking out!"

"Because you want him to ask you or because you don't want him to ask you?" Cozy asked—even though she already knew the answer.

"You dork! You know I'm totally in love with Dylan Hill," Ashley giggled.

Cozy smiled. "I know you are, and I'm sure he'll ask you...especially if you wear my pink sweater. It's my good luck sweater."

"I know, huh?" Ashley giggled. "Thanks, Cozy," she said.

"You're welcome," Cozy laughed. "Now close the door. I've got the breakfast shift again tomorrow."

"Okay. Love you."

"Love you too, Ash."

Ashley closed the door, and Cozy sighed. Setting her journal and pen on the nightstand, she turned off her reading lamp.

"Wonderful," she whispered, punching her pillow. "My sixteen-year-old sister and my *grandmother* have more exciting lives than I do."

Cozy closed her eyes and tried not to think of

the mountain of ornaments she still needed to finish by the end of the week. She giggled then, however—smiled at the memory of the look of delight on her grandma's face when Cozy had suggested that Mr. Buckly Bryant might be a good kisser. It had been a precious expression—purely precious! As she struggled to settle all the thoughts bouncing around in her head, Cozy found herself wondering if her grandma's new neighbor really was a good kisser.

CHAPTER TWO

"Oh! They're so adorable, Cozy," Mindy exclaimed. Cozy smiled when her friend gasped as she opened another box to view the delicately crafted ornament inside. "I mean, seriously…these are your best ones yet!"

"Anybody can crack a walnut open and make them, Mindy," Cozy said. "You're so dramatic."

"I'm so serious!" Mindy assured her with further theatrics. "Maybe anybody can make a walnut ornament…but nobody can make them like this! If anybody could, you wouldn't be raking in so much cash, and you know it." Mindy's smile broadened as she opened the next box. "Ooooh, I should've ordered more!"

"No way, Mindy," Cozy argued. "You've already spent way, way too much. I feel like a total loser for even taking your money."

"Hey!" Mindy said, wagging a scolding index finger at Cozy. "Knock it off! Girl, your ornaments are the best bang for the buck in town. You wouldn't be burning the midnight oil so often if they weren't."

"Well, if you're happy with them…then I'll try to deal with being a dumb walnut peddler," Cozy giggled.

"I love them, and you know it!" Mindy's brow wrinkled, her lips pursing as she cooed, "Oooh, how cute! Look at the little teeny weenie lamb gazing at the manger. They're *so* cute!"

"And you're so funny," Cozy said, still smiling.

"Did you give one like this to your grandma this year?" Mindy asked.

"Yeah. She loved it! I think maybe it was her favorite of the ones I made for her."

"And look at the tiny little baby Jesus," Mindy gasped. "Oh, Cozy…I *love* this one. Thank you so much!"

"Thank *you*, Mindy," Cozy said. "You're always so supportive…and not just where my stupid ornaments are concerned."

Mindy looked to Cozy, her eyes twinkling with merriment.

"I'm your friend, Cozy," she said. "It comes naturally, right?"

Cozy nodded. "Yeah."

Again Mindy looked to the boxes of ornaments sitting on the kitchen table of her apartment. "Seriously, Coze, these are great! I totally love them," she said, tucking the nativity walnut back into its box. "So you're going to your grandma's tonight again?"

"Yeah. I just need some space," Cozy sighed. "You know I love my brothers and sisters…but I'm telling you, the boys are driving me crazy!"

"Little brothers are like that," Mindy agreed. "And with three little brothers, I'm surprised you're not pulling your hair out. What are they up to now?"

"Hidden video cameras in our rooms," Cozy said, shaking her head. "They don't think about what they might catch—you know, like Ashley or Mayree changing clothes and stuff." She paused and giggled. "Though Tony did catch Ashley playing with her old Barbie dolls. He's merciless in teasing her about it."

Mindy shrugged. "I still have all my Barbies. I get them out once in a while…just to make sure they're okay."

"Me too," Cozy agreed. "But you know Ashley. She's at the everything-is-so-embarrassing stage. I even told her that I still get my Barbies out and that I think a girl should never completely give them up…but she still chased Tony around the house screaming at him and then cried for an hour."

"Poor thing," Mindy mumbled with a pouty lower lip of compassion.

"Who? Ashley or Tony?" Cozy asked with amused sarcasm.

"But seriously…no woman should ever give up her Barbies. Not completely."

"I know," Cozy said. "Still, I like the way they *used* to make them though—you know, when they had bigger busts and skinnier waists. I don't care if it wasn't realistic. I like the wasp-waist look the older Barbies had."

"Me too," Mindy emphatically agreed. "And now

the old clothes don't fit the new Barbies, and the new clothes don't fit the old Barbies. Man, they just jacked everything up when they changed her measurements."

"Totally," Cozy sighed.

"And don't even get me started on Ken," Mindy added, shaking her head with disgusted disapproval.

"Oh, I know, huh?"

Mindy laughed. "Look at us. We're only twenty-one, and we're already talking about the good old days."

"That's because we need to get lives," Cozy suggested, still smiling.

"Yeah. Working at the café doesn't lend itself to too much free time," Mindy sighed. "And then *you* spend the rest of *your* time digging the guts out of walnuts and painting them."

Cozy shrugged. "There's nothing else to do," she said. "Sometimes it seems like all the old-school masculine types I daydream about disappeared about the same time Barbie's chest got smaller. You know?"

"Yeah. But I think it's more like they're just—you know—hidden. Like they're here…but it's just not as obvious as it used to be, and you have to look harder for them."

Cozy nodded. "Kind of like those hidden picture books where you have to find the guy in the red-and-white striped shirt."

"Exactly!" Mindy affirmed. "Or those pictures you have to stare at and go cross-eyed over before you see the three-dimensional thing."

Cozy glanced at the clock on Mindy's microwave.

"Oh! I've gotta go. I told Grandma I'd be over by four."

"Okay," Mindy said, offering a friendly embrace. "Have fun. Enjoy your peace and quiet."

"Oh, I will," Cozy said, returning Mindy's hug.

"And look at it this way. You're almost done with walnuts for this year," Mindy chirped.

"I know!" Cozy sighed. "I can hardly stand to eat them anymore…though I still like my Grandma's banana nut bread."

"Oh, me too. That stuff is heaven!"

Cozy smiled and headed for the door. "Okay. I'll see you at work."

"For sure. Bye."

"Bye."

Cozy giggled as she hurried toward her car. Mindy was always so funny. She loved the random venue their conversations often took. The truth was Cozy liked close, intimate relationships. She wasn't one to sit around wishing she had tons of casual friends. She liked her family—even if her siblings did drive her crazy sometimes—her mom and dad, her grandparents. Beyond that, Cozy Robbins had always been happiest with just a few loyal, cherished friends. She valued her relationships with those she loved and was perfectly content in them—almost perfectly content anyway. There was one other relationship she longed for: the romantic kind, the passionate love kind. Still, she tried not to obsess over it. After all, she was getting a good education and planning for her future. She just wished there was someone she could share that future with—and not just anyone—the right one.

Oh, Cozy had certainly heard a ton of lectures on not setting her sights on, or expecting to find, just her one and only meant-to-be soul mate—and in truth, she thoroughly believed two people could fall in love without having been predestined to do so. Yet in the deepest feelings of her own heart, she knew she was different. Cozy knew that the man she needed—the man who would make her happiness complete—needed to be of a similar character as she. Not that he shouldn't be social—it was important that he was—but she needed a man who didn't hold his social life as his highest priority. *She* wanted to be his priority—because she knew he would be hers. Though she was very guarded about the true feelings of her heart, Cozy knew that when she fell in love—really fell in love—the love she owned would be overpowering, almost debilitating in a way. And love like that needed reciprocation. Her parents were that way—seemed absolutely made for each other—and that's what Cozy wanted. It was what she needed. She had never verbalized her feelings on the matter to anyone other than her Grandma Robbins. It was a secret understanding of herself that she kept safely hidden away, for it was just the type of thing to spur teasing from others. She doubted most people would even understand the depth of her emotions on the matter. They'd certainly say she didn't have enough experience or was too young to understand the reality of it all. But Cozy knew the truth—because Cozy had always known exactly who she was.

As she drove over the bridge spanning the river, she noticed that in just the few days since she'd last seen her Grandma, the leaves of the cottonwood trees had turned wholly gold. They were beautiful! She would need to take a walk down by the river that very week if she wanted to enjoy their brilliance before the first freeze settled in and tainted the cottonwood leaves' bright gold to dull brown.

She turned on the car radio and smiled when she heard that 95.1 FM had begun to play Christmas music already. Sure, it wasn't even mid-November yet, but Cozy didn't mind. Grouchy old humbugs did, but she didn't. To Cozy Robbins, Christmas was something that should be considered, appreciated, and enjoyed throughout the year. And besides, it was a wonderful scene to behold, driving beneath a canopy of fresh yellow leaves with Mannheim Steamroller's rendition of "Bring a Torch, Jeanette, Isabelle" wafting through the car.

"Grandma?" Cozy called as she closed the front door behind her. She inhaled a deep breath, bathing in the warm, inviting scent of banana nut bread baking in the oven. "Grandma? Are you in here?"

"Cozy!" her grandma called in a loud whisper. "I'm in the kitchen. Hurry!"

Cozy frowned, and her heart leapt as worry consumed her for a moment. Yet as she hurried to the kitchen to find her grandma kneeling at the window that faced the new neighbor's yard and peering out with a pair of binoculars, she exhaled a sigh of relief.

"Grandma! You're still spying on him?" she giggled.

"Get down! They'll see us. Get down!" Dottie ordered in a whisper, waving one hand in a gesture that Cozy should duck.

Giggling with amusement at her grandma's latest antics, Cozy dropped to her hands and knees and crawled toward the window.

"Who'll see us?" she asked.

"Here," Dottie whispered, pausing only long enough to reach for a second set of binoculars sitting on the nearby counter. "These are for you." She smiled at Cozy and winked as a grin of mischief spread over her face. "And now, may I present the entertainment for this evening—Mr. Buckly 'Hunk of Burning Love' Bryant...and company."

"And company?" Cozy asked, accepting the binoculars. Slowly she rose to her knees, peering through the binoculars as she began to adjust them. Mr. Bryant came into focus. He was raking more leaves, but this time he had assistance. Cozy felt her mouth drop open—audibly gasped at the sight of the man helping him.

"I know!" Dottie whispered. "Va va va voom, right?"

"Holy cow!" Cozy exclaimed as she adjusted the binoculars further. "Who *is* that?"

"I have no idea," Dottie answered. "But he's

something you don't see every day, right? I knew you'd like him."

Cozy watched as the man, much younger than Mr. Bryant, picked up another piece of wood and set it on a chopping stump. Adeptly wielding an ax, he split the wood right down the middle. Cozy watched as he picked up the newly split pieces of firewood and tossed them aside. He then retrieved another large piece of wood and repeated the process.

The man splitting the wood had discarded his shirt somewhere, providing a perfect view of the sculpted muscles of his back and arms to Cozy and her grandma. His jeans were worn, as were his work boots. He wore a baseball cap with the bill turned backward.

"Is he cute?" Cozy asked her grandma in a whisper.

"Cosette Robbins!" Dottie giggled. "What kind of a question is that? Isn't it obvious that he's cute?"

Cozy adjusted the binoculars again as she peered out through the window to the man chopping wood next door. "I can't see his face. Who cares if he's all muscles and stuff if he isn't cute?"

At that moment, however, the man turned, removing his cap and raking a hand through his dark hair. Cozy and her grandmother gasped in unison as they gazed at the handsome face of the muscular woodchopper.

"Like I said...va va va voom!" Dottie whispered.

"Add a double voom to that, Grandma," Cozy agreed with a giggle. She paused, still smiling as she asked, "How long have you been spying on them, Grandma?"

Dottie shrugged. "About ten minutes, I guess." She exhaled a breathy laugh. "I was waiting for my second batch of banana bread to finish when I happened to glance out the window and see them out there working. It's killing my knees, of course...but some things are worth the pain."

"Wait a minute," Cozy said then, looking to her grandma. "Do you mean to tell me you haven't been over there yet? I thought you were going to bake banana bread a couple of days ago and take it over."

Dottie looked to her granddaughter and shrugged. "I couldn't get up the nerve," she confessed. "But I figured, since you were going to be over here tonight... we could go together."

"What?" Cozy exclaimed. "Grandma! I am not going over there. Not while Mr. Sexy Flexy is visiting."

"Oh, come on, Cozy," Dottie said. "We'll just take the banana nut bread over—you know, like you said we should—as a housewarming sort of welcome-to-the-neighborhood offering, and then we'll just be on our way."

"I said *you* should take banana nut bread over... not *we*," Cozy reminded. "Anyway, he's your neighbor, not mine."

"Oh, come on, Cozy," Dottie said, returning her attention to the men in the backyard next door. "Don't you want to get a real good look at that young man?

Anyway, you know what they say. What's good for the grandma is good for the granddaughter."

"That's not what they say, Grandma," Cozy argued, peering through her own binoculars once more.

"Well, it still applies here."

"The only thing that applies here is that we're acting like stalkers," Cozy mumbled as she watched Mr. Bryant talking to the young man. "Besides, they're out in the backyard working. How dumb would it look for us to just walk up and say, 'Hi! Here's some banana nut bread'?"

"We'll wait until they go in...then we'll go over there," Dottie answered.

"What are we supposed to do until then? Kneel here just staring out the window at them?"

Dottie looked to Cozy, smiling. "Do you have something better to do? I thought you were coming over to relax. What's more relaxing than a stakeout?"

Cozy giggled and shook her head. "Well, I'll say this, Grandma. You're a whole lot more fun than most grandmas I know."

"Thank you, sweet pea," Dottie said, adjusting her binoculars. "Oh, look! My hunk of burning love is back to raking leaves, and your sexy flexy is helping him." They were both silent for a moment as they studied the goings-on in the neighbor's yard. "Hmmm. Do you think Mr. Bryant hired him or that he's a relative?"

"He looks too young to be Mr. Bryant's son," Cozy offered. "But then again...you never know."

At that very moment, both men turned to look in

the direction of Dottie's house—in the direction of the very kitchen window where Cozy and her grandmother kneeled in spying.

"Oh, shoot!" Dottie exclaimed as she quickly ducked down below the windowsill.

Cozy gasped and ducked too. "Do you think they saw us?" she asked. "How embarrassing!"

But Dottie shook her head. "No. We were quick enough." She smiled, then giggled, and burst into laughter.

Cozy couldn't help but laugh too. It was absurd! The whole thing was goofy, and Cozy and her grandmother continued to laugh themselves to tears.

When they finally did settle down, Dottie sighed, "Oh, my sweet baby girl! I haven't laughed like that for so long. It felt wonderful."

"It did," Cozy agreed, wiping the tears from her eyes. She looked to her Grandma and hugged her where they sat on the floor in the kitchen under the window. "I needed a good laugh too."

The oven timer began to sound, and Cozy helped her grandma to her feet. "We'll let the new loaves cool for an hour or two, and then we'll take them over to Mr. Bryant. If we're lucky, maybe his company will still be there too."

"Grandma—" Cozy began to argue.

"Meanwhile," Dottie interrupted, however, "I picked up some new crackle-glass votives for you, angel. You are going to love these new ones. They are so pretty!"

"You didn't have to buy any more for me, Grandma," Cozy said. "I don't even have a place of my own. You shouldn't—"

"Oh, you have to have them, Cozy," Dottie argued. "And besides...you'll have a place of your own someday. And a girl can never have too many crackle-glass candle implements."

"But—"

"And don't worry, I picked up plenty for Ashley and Mayree too. Oh, and some I think your mother will die for."

Cozy sighed and shook her head. There was no stopping her grandmother when she put her mind to something. And besides, Cozy did love crackle glass. To her, there was almost nothing in the world as serene as sitting in a cozy room with the lights off and nothing but the flicker of the candles in crackle-glass votive and pillar holders. To Cozy, crackle glass lent an atmosphere of mystery to the ambiance of a comfy room. The process of immersing molten hot glass into cold water to purposely crack it was a centuries-old craft. Glassblowers then reheated the glass to mold it into the desired shape and seal the cracks. It was a fascinating process to Cozy, and the end result was one of her very favorite things to enjoy. She preferred to set several crackle-glass votives on her nightstand next to the wall at night. That way, as the candle flame flickered inside, the cracks in the glass cast lacy shadows on the wall. It was beautiful. So even though Cozy had begun to scold her grandma for buying more of the lovely novelty votives for her, she was glad she had, for her grandma was right—a girl could never have too many crackle-glass implements.

"Now, these are yours," Dottie began, separating several small boxes from a pile of others in the center of the table. "You'll love this design! Pinecones and fir sprigs with gold embellishments."

Cozy smiled as she opened one of the boxes. Her grandma was so darling—so very precious. She thought of having entered the house to find her staking out the new neighbor. What a jewel! She sighed, thinking the least she could do was to find the courage to help her meet Mr. Bryant—the hunk of burning love, as her Grandma called him. A little wave of anxiety rolled her in stomach at the thought of meeting whoever the young man helping him with his yard work was, however. She hoped the half-naked woodchopper was gone by the time the banana bread had cooled.

"And just look at this, Cozy!" Dottie exclaimed as she unwrapped a stemmed votive holder. "Isn't it just gorgeous?"

"It's beautiful," Cozy agreed as she studied the beautiful piece of glasswork. "Thank you so much, Grandma. You know I love them, don't you?"

Dottie smiled. "Of course! No matter how you argue with me about buying them for you...I know you love when I do."

Cozy giggled as her grandma handed her another votive holder to inspect.

❧

"Grandma...I-I don't really want to do this," Cozy whispered as Dottie reached out to ring Mr. Bryant's doorbell several hours later.

"Of course you do," Dottie whispered in return. "After all...it was your idea."

Cozy rolled her eyes. She could only hope the naked woodchopper had left. She and her grandmother had gotten busy with Thanksgiving and Christmas plans and had completely forgotten to spy out the window to see if he'd left the house after helping Mr. Bryant in his backyard.

Her breath caught in her throat, however, as Mr. Bryant's front door opened to reveal none other than the handsome woodchopper standing before them. At least he was now wearing a T-shirt—and Cozy was glad of it.

"Hello," Dottie said, offering a hand to the super-handsome young man.

The man grinned and shook her grandma's hand. "Hello," he greeted. His voice was deep and rich, like liquid cloves.

"I'm Dottie Robbins," Dottie began, "and this is my granddaughter Cozy. We've come to welcome Mr. Bryant to the neighborhood."

"Well, that's really nice," the man said, smiling. "Come on in. I'll go get him."

"Thank you," Dottie said.

Cozy followed her grandmother into the house and

forced a nervous grin when the handsome woodchopper smiled at her and said, "Hi there."

"Hi," she managed.

"Have a seat, ladies," the man said. "He's just in the back." The man turned then, calling, "Grandpa... you've got company."

As the man strode away down the hallway, Dottie whispered, "Grandpa, is it? Well, that makes more sense than anything in the entire world, doesn't it? Did you see those baby blues on that boy?"

"Yes," Cozy whispered. She certainly had seen the man's eyes. They were fascinating—exactly the color of a cloudless October sky.

"The apple usually doesn't fall too far from the tree...even grand-apples, I guess," Dottie whispered.

"They're going to hear you, Grandma!" Cozy scolded in a giggle. For all her nervousness, she was excited too. It would be fun to see her Grandma interact with Mr. Bryant—not to mention how enjoyable it would be to steal another peek at his handsome woodchopping grandson.

"It's a very tidy home...especially for an older, single man," Dottie commented as she glanced about the entryway and into the family room to their left.

Cozy followed her gaze, smiling when she saw a warm fire burning in the hearth in the comfortable-looking room.

Mr. Bryant appeared then, smiling at Cozy's grandmother as he approached. "Well, good evening there, Mrs. Robbins," he greeted. "I was hoping we'd run into one another again soon. I almost sent Jesse over to borrow a ladder this afternoon, but he found mine buried out in the garage."

Cozy's own smile broadened, for it was obvious the man was sincerely pleased at seeing her grandma.

"Well, I'm glad you found yours, Mr. Bryant," Dottie began, "but you feel free to borrow anything you need from me. That's what neighbors are for, after all."

"Thank you, Mrs. Robbins," Mr. Bryant chuckled. "I see you've met my grandson Jesse already."

"Jesse Bryant," the grandson added.

"Yes, we did," Dottie confirmed, nodding to the handsome woodchopper. Looking to Cozy, she said, "And this is my granddaughter Cozy. It's Cosette, actually…but she prefers Cozy."

Mr. Bryant offered his hand to Cozy, and she accepted it. "It's nice to meet you, Cozy," he said.

"You too," she said, smiling.

Mr. Bryant looked from Dottie to Cozy and back. "And what brings you ladies out tonight?"

"We just wanted to welcome you to the neighborhood," Dottie answered. "I baked some banana bread earlier, and we thought you might enjoy a little something yummy."

Dottie nudged Cozy with her elbow.

"Oh!" Cozy exclaimed, having completely forgotten that she was the one holding the two small loaves of bread. "Here you go," she said, offering the loaves to Mr. Bryant.

"I'll take them," Jesse said.

Cozy was mortified when she felt her hands trembling as she handed the bread loaves to Mr. Bryant's grandson. She hated the fact that good-looking men made her jittery, but for some reason they did. Furthermore, Jesse Bryant was extraordinarily good-looking—almost sinfully so. She watched as he placed the loaves on top of a small bookcase situated nearby.

"Well, come on in and sit a spell, ladies," Mr. Bryant said, motioning toward the comfortable room nearby. "You can't come bearing gifts and not sit down for a minute."

"Well, we really should be getting back to—" Cozy began, wanting only to escape.

"We'd love to visit!" Dottie interrupted, however. "If it wouldn't be an imposition, that is."

"Of course not," Mr. Bryant assured her.

Cozy watched Mr. Bryant stride into the room— watched her grandma follow. She paused, still uncertain that they should indeed linger, but when Jesse Bryant gestured that she should precede him, she nodded and stepped in.

"Have a seat," Mr. Bryant said, pointing to a sofa near the fire as he sat down in a worn lounge chair opposite them. Jesse Bryant simply sat down on the floor, leaned back on one elbow, and stretched his long legs out over the carpet.

"Jesse helped me get the fireplace and chimney all cleaned up today," Mr. Bryant said. "We chopped some wood and got some leaves raked."

"It sounds like you're settling right in," Dottie chirped.

"Yep. Nice and cozy," Mr. Bryant agreed.

Cozy smiled, for she had not missed the twinkle in Mr. Bryant's eyes that was mirroring the one in her grandma's. She hadn't seen such pink color in her grandma's cheeks for years either. Mr. Bryant and her grandma were definitely attracted to one another, and it made Cozy's heart swell with delight.

Mr. Bryant's house smelled like cedar and furniture polish. Cozy's smile broadened as she thought of how entirely masculine the atmosphere was. Her grandma was right—it was a very tidy home.

Rather inadvertently, she glanced to Jesse Bryant. Her heart fluttered a little as she noticed the knowing grin lingering on his handsome face as he too seemed to be aware of the invisible sparks flying back and forth between their grandparents. He appeared to be as amused and pleased as Cozy felt, and she was glad. Though it was somewhat difficult to imagine her grandma harboring a crush on someone, it would be a wonderful thing for her.

Cozy began to imagine all kinds of scenarios then— such as the possibility of her grandma and Mr. Bryant truly falling in love. He seemed to be a very nice man. He was well-mannered and polite—and handsome. Still, Cozy knew she shouldn't hope for too much. Chances were slim that they would be so perfectly matched as to find instant joy with one another. Yet, at the same time, she thought that perhaps a little nurturing of the idea on her part couldn't hurt too much.

"Do you live nearby, Jesse?" Cozy heard her grandma inquire.

"Yes, ma'am," Jesse answered. "Not too far away... about four miles."

"Oh, that's so good," Dottie said. Returning her attention to Mr. Bryant, she said, "I don't know what I'd do if I didn't have family close."

"Me neither," Mr. Bryant said. He looked to his grandson and smiled. "Jesse's a good man. I appreciate him more than he knows."

Jesse nodded, implying that he appreciated his grandfather just as much.

"So you live nearby too, Cozy?" Mr. Bryant asked.

"I live up on the west side," Cozy answered. She was beginning to relax a little. "But it's not too far."

"I like it up there too. But I can tell I'm gonna love it down here by the river," Mr. Bryant sighed. "I don't know why I waited so long to move."

"Oh, it's just wonderful down here! I've lived in this area...oh, almost fifty years. I could never leave," Dottie said.

"Well, I certainly hope not," Mr. Bryant said, winking at Dottie. "After all, good neighbors are hard to come by these days."

"Yes, they are," Dottie giggled.

Instinctively, Cozy looked to Jesse. He was looking at her, the same knowing grin on his face. His eyebrows arched slightly as if to say, *Are you seeing what I'm seeing?*

and Cozy smiled, offering a slight nod of assurance.

"I'm assuming you're retired, Mrs. Robbins," Mr. Bryant said.

"Dottie...please call me Dottie," Dottie said.

Mr. Bryant smiled, nodded, and said, "I'm assuming you're retired, Dottie."

"Yes and no," Dottie answered. "I was fortunate enough to be a wife and mother...and now a grandmother. So my children are grown, yes. But my grandchildren...well, that's still a job."

Mr. Bryant chuckled. "Yes, it is. Indeed it is." He looked to Cozy then, and she fancied his eyes bathed her in the sensation that he could look right through a person. "And how about you, Cozy? What do you do?"

Cozy shrugged. "Well, right now I still have two semesters of college before I'll have my degree. So I work at the Morning Star Café on the west side."

"Waitress?" he asked.

"Yes."

"That's a rough job."

"Sometimes. But the tips are pretty good there," Cozy explained.

"And she's an artisan!" Dottie added, smiling proudly.

"Really?" Mr. Bryant asked, his smile broadening.

"No...not really," Cozy said as she felt a blush rise to her cheeks. She playfully glared at her grandmother.

"Yes, you are, sweet pea!" Dottie corrected. Looking to Mr. Bryant, she said, "Cozy makes Christmas tree ornaments. They're quite the trendy little novelty."

Frowning with curiosity, she looked to Cozy once more and asked, "How many orders did you end up filling this year?"

"Seven hundred," Cozy answered. Looking to Mr. Bryant, however, she shook her head and said, "It's really nothing to speak of."

"Sure it is!" Dottie argued enthusiastically. She looked back to Mr. Bryant, saying, "She's paid for four semesters of college tuition with her little walnut ornaments."

"Really?" Jesse Bryant asked. He wore an expression of being impressed.

"W-well, yes…but it's really nothing," Cozy stammered.

"It doesn't sound like nothing," Mr. Bryant chuckled.

"I keep telling her she should be proud of what she's done with them," Dottie said. "But for some reason, she likes to keep it a secret most of the time."

"Well, now I'm curious," Mr. Bryant said.

"Me too," Jesse agreed.

"Do you have any with you?" Mr. Bryant asked.

"Um…no. I don't really carry them around," Cozy answered. She could feel her face turning redder and redder. She couldn't believe her grandmother had brought up the subject of her ornaments.

"Well, I'd like to see one next time you're over at your grandmother's," Mr. Bryant said.

"Really?" Cozy asked. "But…they're kind of a girl thing. The only men I sell to are usually buying them for the wives and girlfriends and stuff."

"Men like Christmas too," Mr. Bryant teased with a wink. "In fact, Jesse here does my Christmas lights every year. He's an electrician, you know, and a master at lighting a house up for the holidays. My place won the neighborhood lighting award for four years running."

"Wow, really?" Cozy asked, smiling at Jesse.

"Yep," he confirmed with a nod.

"Oh, I haven't had lights up for years," Dottie wistfully sighed. "Not since my husband died."

"Well, we can't have that, Dottie," Mr. Bryant said. "I'm sure Jesse here would be willing to put up a few lights for you too. Wouldn't you, Jesse?"

"Of course," Jesse agreed.

"Oh, no! I couldn't ask you do to that," Dottie argued.

"You didn't ask me," Jesse said. "I volunteered. I'll be over here half a day doing Grandpa's...so I can toss a few strings up for you too, if you like."

"Really? That would be so wonderful!" Dottie exclaimed.

"Grandma...you can't ask him to—" Cozy began.

"Oh, let him do it," Mr. Bryant said. "He doesn't have anything better to do that day, right, Jesse?"

"Right," Jesse confirmed.

"Well, I'm sure that's not true, Mr. Bryant...but—" Dottie began.

"Buck," Mr. Bryant interrupted.

Cozy stifled a giggle as she saw her grandma blush

with delight. "Buck. I'm sure he's got plenty of other things needing his time and attention."

"Nope. He'll do your lights. He'd love to," Buck assured her.

"Well, then I'd love to have him do it!" Dottie chirped.

Cozy smiled as she looked to Jesse to see him shrug broad shoulders. He winked at her, and she understood he was as amused as she was at the way their grandparents had assigned his time and labor with very little input from him.

"I guess we should be going," Dottie said then. "We don't want to overstay our welcome."

"Oh, I don't think that would be possible," Buck flirted, winking at Dottie.

Cozy giggled when her grandma blushed again.

"You're very kind, Buck. But I promised Cozy some peace and quiet tonight before she goes home...so we better get back."

Cozy stood as her grandmother did. She was impressed when both men politely rose to their feet as well.

"Let me get the door for you," Jesse said, striding toward the entryway.

"Come over any time the thought strikes you, Dottie," Buck said, offering Dottie his hand.

Dottie blushed again as she took his hand and said, "Thank you."

"You too, Cozy," Buck said, nodding to Cozy.

"Thank you," she said.

"It was nice to meet you, Mrs. Robbins," Jesse said as Dottie started out the door.

"Oh now, you call me Dottie," she said, playfully patting the younger man on one broad shoulder.

"Yes, ma'am," Jesse chuckled. He turned to Cozy then, smiled a smile of pure masculine allure, and said, "Nice to meet you too."

"Have a good evening," Cozy managed to answer as she followed her grandmother over the threshold.

"Good night, ladies," Buck called after them.

"Thank you. You too," Dottie called over her shoulder as she and Cozy turned left on the sidewalk.

"Cozy," Dottie began as Cozy took her arm as they walked.

"Yes?" Cozy asked. She seemed to know what was coming next, and a giggle tickled her throat.

"I think I'm in love!" Dottie sighed. "I have butterflies in my stomach. Real butterflies! I haven't had butterflies in years and years."

Cozy laughed. "He's quite dashing, Grandma. And I think he likes you too."

"Do you really think so?"

Cozy nodded. "Yes. It's obvious."

Dottie smiled, glanced to Cozy a minute with an expression of suspicion, and asked, "And what do you think of that grandson of his? Quite the dreamboat, isn't he."

"*Quite* the dreamboat," Cozy agreed. Still, she wanted to change the subject. She knew exactly what her grandma was thinking and knew she couldn't allow her to keep thinking it. Her grandmother was thinking Mr. Bryant's handsome grandson would be the perfect match for Cozy. She always thought any good-looking twenty-something would be the perfect match for her, and Cozy didn't want her getting her hopes up again. "Is everyone coming for Thanksgiving this year, Grandma?" she asked in an effort to divert the course of their conversation.

"Not quite everyone," Dottie answered, having taken the bait. "I haven't heard from your Aunt Carol as to whether they'll be able to make it."

"Well, I'm excited either way," Cozy said. "I swear...why is it people only make pumpkin pie at Thanksgiving and Christmas? I'm salivating just thinking about it."

"Me too," Dottie said. "Me too."

Dottie glanced to Cozy as they entered the house together. She knew exactly what Cozy was doing— avoiding conversation about Buck Bryant's handsome grandson, that's what. But Dottie Robbins was not one to be so easily dissuaded. She liked the look of that young man—liked the character he showed by being so loyal and helpful to his grandfather. It was high time Cozy had some excitement and romance. She spent far too much time agonizing over money and school. She needed a handsome boyfriend to level everything out for her—to give some balance to her life. With any luck, Dottie figured she might be able to put Jesse Bryant in Cozy's way enough to have her stumble right into some. He didn't look married—wore no wedding ring. Dottie had been sure to notice. Furthermore, it seemed he had extra time on his hands. If he had time to put up Christmas lights on not only his grandfather's house but Dottie's as well, then the young man needed something in his life too.

"Let's have us a couple of slices of banana bread, shall we?" Dottie asked, closing the front door behind her and Cozy.

"Definitely!" Cozy exclaimed.

"All right then. You slice a few pieces for us, and I'll light some of the new votives on the mantel. Oh! And flip on the stereo too, Cozy. Something soothing, okay?"

"Okay, Grandma," Cozy agreed.

Dottie sighed as she went to the small table in the dimly lit family room at the front of the house and retrieved a box of matches from the drawer in it. Yep, Cozy needed some romance—and Dottie decided then and there that maybe Jesse Bryant would be just the right man to fit the bill. After all, he didn't look like a psychopathic killer or some hit man for the mob.

"So I'm thinking you like that little lady," Jesse suggested as his grandfather watched through a slit in the curtains of the entryway as the lady next door and her granddaughter walk up the sidewalk.

"You're thinking right, boy," Buck chuckled.

"Well, we better see if her banana bread is any good then," Jesse said, picking up one of the small loaves of bread he'd placed on the bookcase in the entryway. Removing the plastic wrap, he simply tore the loaf of sweet bread in half, handing one half to his grandfather.

Buck bit into the bread and smiled. "Yep. She bakes a mean banana bread," he mumbled.

Jesse laughed as he took a bite. He felt his own eyebrows arch in approval.

"I guess the jury's in then, Grandpa," he said.

"I think so," Buck chuckled.

Jesse couldn't keep from smiling. The light in his grandfather's eyes was brighter than he'd seen it in years. Maybe this Dottie Robbins would keep it there. He'd been worried about having talked his grandfather into selling the old house and moving down to the valley. He knew it wasn't always a good thing for older people to relocate. Still, Jesse had hoped the change would help pull his grandpa out of the sadness he'd dipped into over and over again since his grandmother had passed away. It looked to be helping too, though Jesse wondered for a moment whether it was really the move that had caused the change in Buck or the presence of the sassy little neighbor lady.

"She's got a pretty granddaughter too," Jesse offered. "And you've always wanted a granddaughter to fuss over."

"I have, haven't I?" Buck chuckled.

Jesse nodded. "Yes, you have." He was hopeful in his grandfather's good mood. He'd definitely take an extra day off work to put up Dottie Robbins's Christmas lights—especially if it meant his grandpa could be over visiting with her while he did it.

Suddenly, he frowned a moment. "Grandpa... did she say her granddaughter paid for college making *walnut* ornaments?"

"I think she did say walnuts," Buck confirmed.

"Must be some fancy walnuts," Jesse mumbled, taking another bite of banana nut bread. He smiled as he chewed, wondering if the walnuts in the banana bread had any relationship to the ones the girl had used to pay for college.

CHAPTER THREE

"Yep. Rosemary and I raised the boy from a pup," Buck said as he sat at Dottie's kitchen table enjoying a mug of mulled cider. "Our oldest boy, Jerry, and his wife, Jesse's parents, were killed in a car accident when Jesse was fifteen. His brothers were much older than Jesse—already in college, all three of them. Me and Rosemary were named as guardians in the will." Buck paused. He smiled, but Dottie knew his heart was aching for his lost wife and son. She thought of her own beloved Marvin. She still missed him.

"But if you ask me, Jesse's turned out better than any of his brothers," Buck sighed. He shook his head. "Those other three…let you me tell you, they need to work on straightening out their priorities a bit. All they want is money, money, and more stuff. But Jesse…he's different. Believe me, he's ambitious enough. He's got a very successful electrical business of his own. Still, he values people more than money. I like to think he got that from me…but I know its Rosemary's influence on him."

The tale of Buck's oldest son—of Jesse's father and

mother—it was heartbreaking. Still, Dottie knew a person didn't live as long as she and Buck had without knowing loss and pain. She had her own, after all. In that moment, however, she was certainly thankful she'd never had to endure losing a child.

"Well, your wife may have ensured his good character," Dottie said, offering her handsome neighbor a comforting smile, "but it's obvious he gets his charm and good looks from you."

Buck chuckled, and Dottie was delighted at the way he winked at her. "I might just have to start dropping in on you every evening, Dottie Robbins. You sure are good for my self-esteem."

"You can drop in any time you want, Buck. Truly," she told him.

"Be careful what you say, ma'am...because I might just take you up on it."

Dottie giggled, delighted by Buck Bryant's attention and company. He'd stopped in to thank her for the banana bread she and Cozy had taken over to him a few days before. She had invited him in for some cider she had mulling on the stove, and to her utter glee, he'd accepted. Now two hours had passed since they'd sat down at the kitchen table for a visit—and Dottie had relished every minute of it.

She studied him a moment—his mesmerizing blue eyes, the way his silvery hair rather tumbled over his forehead a bit. Oh, he was handsome! His jaw was square and defined, and his smile was purely fascinating. Dottie felt somewhat ridiculous, however, for the goose bumps that periodically rippled over her arms when he looked at her made her feel seventeen again. She kept inwardly scolding herself for the butterflies fluttering about in her stomach, even though she couldn't do a thing to keep them calm.

"So," he began. She fancied that his smile changed a bit—that his eyes flashed with a bit of withheld mischief. "Tell me about this granddaughter of yours. She wouldn't, by any chance, be…available…would she?"

Dottie's smile broadened. She even giggled. Oh, she liked the way this man thought!

"As a matter of fact, she is," she answered.

Buck chuckled, nodded his head with approval, and said, "Go on."

"Well, she's an angel, of course," Dottie began.

"Of course," Buck chuckled.

"She's a thoughtful girl…uncommonly thoughtful," Dottie explained. "She's always worried about someone else…never herself. She's the oldest of six children and obviously very talented, and she's worked very hard to get her education. But if there's one thing that worries me about Cozy, it's that her life is a little unbalanced right now. She's driven to finish college, and that's good. But it seems she doesn't take any time to just… you know…to just *be*."

Again Buck nodded. "I could see that in her the other night when you two brought that bread over."

Dottie smiled. "Yes. She was uncomfortable then." She paused, winking at Buck as she added, "But I do think that had a whole lot more to do with your handsome grandson than she'd ever like to admit."

"Good!" Buck exclaimed, slapping his knee. "Together we've got a good man and a good girl...so let's throw them into the ring together and see what happens."

"So you're not opposed to a little matchmaking adventure, Mr. Bryant?" Dottie asked with a giggle.

"Not in this case, Mrs. Robbins," he assured her.

"I mean, we hardly know each other...yet we're willing to meddle in the lives of our grandchildren? What would people think?"

"Who cares what people think?" he said, smiling at her. "And besides, we've got enough age and experience between us to recognize things most people are too busy to notice. I liked the look of your granddaughter for my boy the minute I saw her. There's a good feeling about her, and I can tell she's the type of girl who can love a man the way he ought to be loved—thoroughly... faults and all."

Dottie nodded. "That's right. That's my Cozy. When she finally allows herself to fall in love, I think it'll be like nothing the world has ever seen."

"Then she's the one for my boy...because he's the same way." Buck paused a moment and seemed deeply thoughtful. "Jesse's a boy who was born in the wrong decade, I think. He'd rather be out chopping wood, rounding up cattle, or some such thing than sitting behind a desk all day. He's a throwback to when physical labor was necessary for survival. He's also got that masculine protective instinct about him that a lot of young women today take offense at."

"Or pretend to take offense at," Dottie interjected.

"Exactly," Buck chuckled. "He needs a girl who'll love all over him, look to him for protection...and still be able to work alongside him when it's necessary."

"Well, you just described my Cozy."

Buck laughed and slapped his knee again. "Then let's do it, Dottie! Let's toss them in the ring together. I got a feeling it'll all work out just fine." He winked, lowered his voice, and added, "And before long, me and you will have a few downright gorgeous little great-grandbabies." Dottie giggled. "Because it seems to me a girl as pretty as your Cozy and a man as handsome as my Jesse...well, that gene pool can't possible fail."

He raised his mug of mulled cider, and Dottie laughed as she clinked hers with it in sealing the deal. "To our new adventure in matchmaking, Mr. Bryant!" she said. "May it be wildly successful."

"And may the end result be not only happiness for our grandkids...but more babies for us to spoil," he finished.

Dottie studied Buck Bryant over the rim of her mug as she sipped her cider. Yep, she liked him! She liked the way he thought—the fact that he was as willing to dive into mischief as she was. Furthermore, she certainly liked the way he looked—the way his blue eyes seemed to pierce right through her skin to her soul. Goose bumps rippled over her arms every time he smiled at her; butterflies swarmed in her stomach whenever he spoke to her. It was wildly invigorating! She thought of Marvin—missed him. She knew she would always miss him. Yet it was good to feel delight once more—pure, tingling delight—and she knew Marvin would understand.

"So what's our first move?" she asked. She would think about Cozy—about the happiness she would know if she and Buck were successful in their endeavors where their grandchildren were concerned.

"Well, when is Cozy planning on visiting you again?" Buck asked.

"This Thursday after work," Dottie answered.

Buck chuckled, his blue eyes fairly flashing with mischief and amusement. "Then I think Thursday would be the perfect day for Jesse to come on over and put up our Christmas lights...don't you?"

Dottie giggled, took a sip of her cider, and, then nodding, said, "Thursday is perfect! We certainly want to make sure our Christmas lights are up before Thanksgiving, now don't we?"

"We certainly do."

"And speaking of Thanksgiving," Dottie ventured, wondering if he would think she was crazy for what she was about to suggest, "do you and Jesse have any plans for Thanksgiving dinner yet?"

Again Buck's eyes glistened with mischief. "Turkey pot pies at my house is all."

"Then...would you like to spend Thanksgiving Day with me and my family here?" Dottie held her breath a moment, her heart hammering with anxiety.

What if he refused? She suddenly knew she would be crushed if he did.

"That would be wonderful, Mrs. Robbins," he said, however, and Dottie sighed with relief. "That is, if you're sure your family wouldn't mind."

"Not at all!" she exclaimed. "They'll love having you."

"Well, I don't know about that...but we'll love being here," he said with a wink.

"Shouldn't you check with Jesse? Make certain it's all right with him to have Thanksgiving with us?" she asked.

"Naw," Buck said. "What man in his right mind would turn down a Thanksgiving dinner with a pretty girl to sit across the table from, in favor of turkey pot pie with his grandpa?"

"Okay then, it's a date," Dottie chirped.

"Oh, I like the sound of that," Buck flirted.

Dottie smiled again, sipped some more cider from her mug, and almost giggled out loud when the old schoolyard song "Sipping Cider through a Straw" began to echo in her mind.

Cozy thought her shift would never end. Of course, anytime she had something fun planned, her time at the café seemed to drag on and on and on. Still, she was finished now and beginning to unwind a bit. Her grandma had called, asking for a few extra Cozy Robbins walnut ornaments to give to friends. It was the same every year. Her grandma would place her order and then a week or two afterwards think of several more people she wanted to give ornaments to. But Cozy had been prepared this year. She had made ten extra ornaments in anticipation of her grandma wanting more. She giggled as she retrieved the basket of extra ornaments from the trunk of the car. She loved her grandma's predictability. It was somehow comforting. A gust of cold wind whipped around her then, and she pulled the hood of her red wool coat up over her head. The temperature was dropping, a sign that winter was on its way. As dry leaves crunched under her feet, a momentary disappointment traveled through her at knowing the beautiful autumn leaves might be gone before Thanksgiving. Still, she loved the holidays, even if they did bring an end to autumn.

"Well, hello there, Little Red Riding Hood."

Cozy gasped, slightly startled by the unexpected voice. Glancing around, she was unsettled—for she couldn't see anyone.

"Up here," the deep, masculine voice called again.

Cozy looked up then and smiled as she saw Jesse Bryant standing on her grandma's roof, stretching out a string of Christmas lights. Already the lower level of her grandma's home was dripping with white icicle lights. It was obvious Jesse was now working on the second story. He looked delicious—absolutely delicious in his jeans, flannel shirt, work boots, and tool belt. He was smiling down at her, and for a moment, Cozy was entirely enchanted—enchanted into silence. He was putting up her grandma's Christmas lights, and something about the fact only added to his attractive appearance. Cozy couldn't quite fathom why—but it did.

"So, you're skipping up to your grandma's house with a basket of goodies?" he asked, still smiling. "Aren't you afraid there might be a wolf waiting inside?"

He chuckled, and his inference finally sunk into Cozy's infatuated mind.

"Oh, I get it," she giggled, glancing down at her red coat. She pushed her hood back from her head. "Ha ha," she added with sarcasm. Jesse Bryant chuckled and shrugged his broad shoulders. "So they've got you slaving away, do they?" she asked. "It's not even Thanksgiving yet."

"Grandpa wanted his lights up before Thanksgiving so he can turn them on Thanksgiving night," he explained. "So I figured I better kill two birds with one stone today."

Cozy's smile broadened. He was so handsome! And so considerate.

"I appreciate that you're doing this for her, you know," she called up to him. "She hasn't had lights on the house since my grandpa died. Thank you."

"You're welcome," he said, still tugging at the string of lights to straighten the wires. "But it's really not a big deal."

"It is to her," she told him. *And to me*, she thought to herself. He simply shrugged once more to indicate he wasn't inconvenienced by putting up Christmas lights for her grandma.

"They're both inside," he said. "You better get in there too. It's cold today. We don't want you catching a cold, now do we?"

"You're not even wearing a coat," she needlessly pointed out. She had the sudden urge to climb up the ladder and throw her arms around him in an effort to warm him. She frowned a little—shook her head at such a ridiculous notion. He was nearly a total stranger! What was wrong with her?

He shrugged again. "I'm a guy. I have more arm and leg hair than you. It keeps me warm."

Cozy giggled. The sleeves of his shirt were rolled up, displaying very muscular forearms that owned no more hair than was average on a man.

"Well, I would certainly hope you have more than me," she teased.

He chuckled, and the sound of it caused goose bumps to race over Cozy's arms. "Go on now. I don't want you to catch cold. And besides, I happen to know your grandma has been waiting all day for you to get here."

"Okay. But be careful up there. I wouldn't want you to fall and get—" she started. She gasped, however, as Jesse began to slip, his arms flailing in an effort to maintain his balance. "Jesse!" she cried as panic leapt into her bosom.

Cozy scowled at him a moment later, however, as he instantly steadied himself and grinned. "That was not funny! You scared me to death," she scolded.

"Sorry," he said. "Kind of."

"Ooo," she playfully growled at him through clenched teeth. "Maybe the wolf is waiting on the roof at grandma's house today, instead of inside."

"Maybe," he chuckled. "Now go on in. It's cold out here."

"Okay. But be careful," she said, wagging an index finger at him.

He nodded, smiling as he returned his attention to the string of lights he'd been stretching.

Cozy climbed the front porch steps to the front door, still smiling as she thought of Jesse Bryant's being kind enough to go to all the trouble of putting lights up for her grandma. He was incredibly kind.

As she entered the house, she was met with the sound of laughter. Setting the basket down, she quickly removed her coat and hung it on one of the coat hooks on the wall. She knew who was laughing, of course—her grandma and Mr. Bryant. Still, she was curious at what found them so mirthful. Retrieving her basket and heading for the kitchen and the source of the merriment, she smiled, thinking how exactly like Red Riding Hood she must've looked to Jesse from his viewpoint on the roof.

"There you are, sweet pea!" Dottie greeted as Cozy entered the kitchen.

"And what's so funny in here?" Cozy asked. "Hello, Mr. Bryant," she offered, nodding to her grandma's guest.

"Hello there, Cozy," Mr. Bryant said, still chuckling.

His blue eyes twinkled with delight, and Cozy couldn't help but giggle a little.

"We were just swapping stories, honey," Dottie said. She stood, drawing Cozy into a warm embrace. "How was work?"

"Crazier than usual, if you can believe that," Cozy sighed, setting her basket down on the table.

"Well, you're here now. Sit down, and I'll get you some cider."

Cozy smiled as she watched her grandma head toward the stove. She could smell the wonderful aroma of the cider and mulling spices simmering there. She frowned again, however, feeling guilty being inside where it was warm and comfortable while Jesse Bryant was out on the roof in the cold breeze.

"He's not wearing a coat, you know," she said.

"Who?" Buck asked.

"Oh, I know it, Cozy," Dottie said, clicking her tongue in tsk-tsking. She shook her head with disapproval as she ladled cider into a mug. "I told him he shouldn't be out there on the roof in this weather without something warmer on."

Buck smiled. "Oh, you mean Jesse. He's fine. He doesn't like to get overheated."

"How long has he been out there, anyway?" Cozy asked, accepting the mug of cider her grandma offered to her.

"It took him about four hours to do my lights," Buck answered. He glanced up to the cuckoo clock on the wall. "I guess he's been over here for about three so far."

"He'll be a Popsicle before he's through," Cozy said. She was worried about Jesse being out in the cold so long.

Buck chuckled. "Well then, you'll just have to warm him up when he comes in," he said, smiling and winking at her. When Cozy sucked in a surprised gasp, he added, "With some of your grandma's cider, of course."

Dottie giggled, and Cozy felt her cheeks grow rosy with a blush of embarrassment as her grandmother winked at her too.

"Now," Buck began, nodding toward Cozy's basket, "are these the extra ornaments you brought for your grandmother?"

"Yes," Cozy answered, feeling somewhat embarrassed as Buck peered into the basket. They were just walnuts, after all.

"I thought Buck might like to have a few for his sisters, honey," Dottie said. "I told him you always keep some extras in reserve for me." She looked to Buck, explaining, "I always order too few, and she ends up having to make more for me."

Cozy was mortified! She felt her cheeks burn crimson.

"Grandma," she scolded in a whisper, "I'm not a little girl selling cookies. You don't have to pressure your friends into—"

"You still don't believe that men like Christmas too, is that it?" Buck chuckled.

"Well…no…that's not it, exactly," Cozy stammered, glaring at her grandma as Buck reached in and removed a white ornament box from the basket. "It's just…well, I can understand putting Christmas lights on the house—that's a manly sort of thing, after all—but walnut ornaments?"

Buck continued to smile and winked at her as he said, "Jesse will be glad to hear you think he's manly."

"Oh, no!" Cozy instantly defended herself. "That's not what I meant."

Buck forced a wounded frown. "You don't think Jesse is manly?" he teased.

"Of course I do," Cozy assured him. "I mean…I don't mean that…I mean…I really don't see why you'd be interested in my ornaments." She glared at her grandma again and added, "Unless you were coerced somehow."

Dottie shook her head, her expression that of innocence. Still, whether or not Dottie had convinced Buck Bryant to look at Cozy's ornaments, she had been the one to bring the stupid subject up in the first place the night they took the banana nut bread over to him.

"Cozy Robbins," Buck chuckled as he looked at the gold embossed logo on top of the little white box. "That's just about the cleverest thing I ever heard."

"Open the box," Dottie urged. Looking to Cozy, she mouthed, *He'll love it!*

Cozy rolled her eyes. She was rather disgusted with

herself for being so nervous. What did it matter if Buck Bryant really liked the ornament or not? Who was he to her? She glanced to her grandma then and saw the spark in her eye as she watched Buck. Sighing, she realized that she secretly hoped Buck Bryant would be her step-grandpa one day.

"Well, look at that," he said as he peered into the box.

"What?" Dottie asked.

"It's a walnut," Buck said, winking to Cozy.

Dottie playfully slapped Buck on one shoulder. "Of course it's a walnut, you ninny," she giggled. "You have to open that one."

Cozy smiled then, delighted with her grandmother's obvious rapture with Buck's presence. She silently scolded herself for being embarrassed that her grandma had brought up the ornaments to Buck. She would do anything to see her grandma happy—even peddle walnut ornaments to men who would most likely rather be tortured and hung from their thumbs.

Buck chuckled as his leathery hands fumbled with the walnut a moment. Fairly quickly, however, he managed to separate the two halves.

"Well, I'll be," he laughed. He looked to Cozy, his blue eyes bright with approval. "Will you look at that. If that isn't the smallest Christmas tree and fireplace I ever saw…then I don't know what is." He continued to chuckle as he studied the tiny Christmas scene set inside the two walnut halves. "I swear, it just draws you in, doesn't it?" he asked, looking to Dottie.

Dottie nodded, and Cozy's smile broadened as she saw her grandma lean closer to Buck as she studied the ornament. Furthermore, Buck seemed truly impressed—sincere in his compliment—and Cozy exhaled the breath she'd been holding.

"I just can't get over it," he said. "Look at those little bitty packages sitting on the rug under the tree." He shook his head, amazed. "Oh, my sister Jenny will flip her wig for this," he laughed. He looked up to Cozy, asking, "What else do you have in that basket, pretty girl?"

Cozy smiled at him. He was a very charming man.

"Why don't you just open a few more and see?" she said.

Buck chuckled, winked at her, and said, "All right, then." He reached into the basket and drew out another little white box.

"What's that?" Dottie said, however.

Cozy listened too, for she'd heard something as well—a child's voice.

"Sounds like a little kid," Buck said, pushing his chair away from the table.

Dottie gasped and exclaimed, "Sounds like he's calling for help!"

Cozy and Dottie hurried after Buck as he swiftly strode to the front door. As he opened the door, they heard a child's voicing crying, "Help me! Help! Anybody! Help me!"

As they stepped out onto the front porch, Cozy gasped as Buck put an arm out to stay her and her grandmother. In the next moment, Jesse dropped down in front of them.

"Did he just jump from the roof?" Dottie asked.

"There," Buck said, pointing in the direction Jesse was running across the street.

Cozy and her grandma simultaneously gasped. A little boy of about four or five had apparently pushed his head between two bars of the old iron fence across the street. It was painfully obvious that he couldn't pull his head back through and was trapped. Cozy rushed passed her grandma and Buck to where Jesse was kneeling down before the sobbing child and trying to soothe him.

"It's all right, buddy," Jesse said in a deep, comforting voice. Again Cozy thought his voice sounded like liquid cloves. "We'll get you out. Don't you worry."

"Should we call someone?" Cozy asked, dropping to her knees.

"Not yet," Jesse said as he studied the situation a minute.

"Tyler!" a woman's voice called out.

Cozy looked to see a young women hurrying toward them.

"Tyler! What in the world were you thinking?" the woman scolded—though Cozy recognized an expression of near panic on her face.

"I wanted to see if my head would fit, Mama," the boy sobbed.

"Oh, honey!" the woman moaned.

"Should we call the fire department?" Dottie asked as she and Buck arrived.

Buck chuckled and shook his head. "Naw. He'll be fine."

"I can free him up pretty easily, ma'am," Jesse said, looking to the worried mother.

"Are you sure?" she asked.

"Yeah," Jesse confirmed. "Is it all right with you if I try?"

"Of course," the young mother assured him.

The boy began to sob, "Help me, mister! I'm too young to die!"

Jesse smiled and tousled the boy's blonde hair. "Oh, you'll be fine. This isn't so bad."

Cozy found that her attention was totally arrested by Jesse in that moment—by his patience and understanding.

"I'm just gonna lift you up, okay, Tyler?" Jesse began as he nimbly hopped the fence. "I'm just gonna lift you up and turn you upside down. Then your ears won't hang up on the bars and your head will slip right out, okay?"

"Are you sure, mister?" the boy cried.

"I'm sure," Jesse chuckled.

"Cozy," Jesse whispered. She looked up to him, and he said, "Just push his head through real gently once I pick him up. Okay?"

"Okay," Cozy said, nodding.

"Are you ready, Tyler?" Jesse asked. Tyler nodded—

sniffled. "Then hang onto the bars at either side of your head for me. Okay?"

Tyler nodded again, and Jesse took hold of the boy at his waist, lifting him until he hung upside down.

"Cozy," Jesse instructed.

Cozy's mouth dropped open in awe as she easily pushed the boy's head through the bars. He was free!

Dottie clapped her hands together with relief, and Buck chuckled as they all watched Jesse hand the traumatized boy to his mother.

"There you go," Jesse said, smiling at Tyler. He reached out and tousled the boy's hair.

"Thanks, mister," Tyler said, rubbing the tears from his eyes.

"You bet," Jesse mumbled.

"Thank you so much," Tyler's mother said. "We just moved in...four houses down. It took Tyler less than an hour to get into trouble."

"Oh, it wasn't too much trouble," Buck said, winking to Tyler.

"I'm Dottie Robbins," Dottie said, offering a hand to the woman.

"Brittany Jackman," the young mother said, accepting Dottie's hand.

"Nice to meet you, Brittany. This is my granddaughter Cozy," Dottie said, looking to Cozy.

"Hi," Cozy greeted.

"And this is our neighbor, Mr. Bryant," Dottie motioned to Buck. "And you've already met your hero, Jesse."

Jesse nodded to the woman. Cozy was instantly disconcerted by the way the young mother's eyes seemed to light up when she looked to Jesse.

"Thank you, Jesse," she said.

"My pleasure," Jesse told her.

Looking back to Dottie, Brittany said, "Tyler and I just moved in. I'm recently divorced, and we thought the change would be good."

"Oh," Dottie said, frowning. "Well, I'm sorry to hear about your divorce…but I'm sure you and Tyler will love this neighborhood."

"I'm sure we will," Brittany said, smiling at Jesse.

Though she didn't quite understand why, Cozy suddenly felt overheated, even for the chill in the late autumn air.

"So, no more sticking your head between things, right, Tyler?" Jesse asked, winking at the boy.

"Never," Tyler sniffled.

"It was nice to meet you," he said.

"You too," Brittany said, gazing at him. Cozy frowned, for the woman was gazing at Jesse—not simply looking at him—gazing at him. "All of you," she added, as if she'd just remembered there were other people standing around.

"Bye-bye," Dottie said. Cozy grinned, knowing full well it was her grandmother's tactful way of dismissing the woman. "Let me know if you need anything, dear."

"Thank you," Brittany said. She *gazed* at Jesse again, adding, "And thank you, again."

"Anytime," Jesse said, smiling at her.

"Come along then," Dottie said, taking Jesse's arm. "We're all going to freeze out here. It was nice to meet you, Brittany."

Cozy almost laughed at her grandmother's sudden possessiveness. It was obvious Dottie Robbins had read Brittany Jackman the same way Cozy had—as having been instantly infatuated with Jesse Bryant.

"Are you almost finished, sweetheart?" Dottie asked Jesse as they all crossed the street together. "I feel awful about you being out here in this cold. Why don't you come in and warm up a bit?"

"I'm almost finished, Mrs. Robbins," Jesse assured her. "Then I'll come in and have some of that cider Grandpa's been raving about, if you wouldn't mind."

"Of course!" Dottie chirped.

"Do you need any help finishing up?" Cozy asked, before she'd even realized the words had tumbled from her mouth. She blushed, thinking how ridiculous she must have sounded.

But Jesse smiled, his sky-blue eyes glistening with pleased amusement.

"No...but thanks for offering," he said. "You all run in and keep warm. I won't be much longer."

"You sure, Jess?" Buck asked.

"Yeah. I'm almost done," he assured his grandpa.

"Well then, come on in and finish sorting through Cozy's ornaments, Buck," Dottie said as they stepped up onto the front porch.

Cozy paused, watching as Jesse climbed the ladder to the roof. She still couldn't believe he'd simply jumped off. Her heart fluttered as she thought of his heroic antics where the little boy was concerned. And they were heroic—leaping from a rooftop and then having the calm logic to know that turning the child upside down would keep his ears from catching on the bars, thereby freeing him. It was impressive, to say the least. Cozy sighed with a delicious delight she wasn't sure she'd ever felt before. She was, however, slightly unsettled by the sudden feelings of heightening intrigue spiraling through her where Jesse Bryant was concerned.

"Focus, Cozy," she whispered as she entered the house. She turned her attention to her grandmother and Buck. They were seated at the table again. "Jesse Bryant is too much twisted steel and sex appeal for you," she mumbled to herself. "Buckly Bryant, however...now he's perfect for your grandma." Resolved to see that her grandmother's happiness was first and foremost, Cozy smiled as she approached the table to see Buck opening another white ornament box.

"Now you tell me, Buck Bryant," Dottie began. "Aren't Cozy's ornaments just the prettiest little things in the whole wide world?"

Buck looked to Dottie and, winking at her, said, "Almost."

Cozy stifled an amused giggle as she saw her grandmother blush and bite her lower lip with delight. She didn't even care if her grandmother had used her silly ornaments as an excuse to get Buck Bryant to her house again. In fact, the thought traveled through her head that she'd only been witness to another life lesson at her grandmother's hand—an example that any trivial thing could be used as a lure when it came to matters of the heart.

CHAPTER FOUR

"You can't be serious, Mr. Bryant," Cozy said, frowning with disbelief. "You can't really want all ten of them. I know you're just being nice…taking pity on a poor college student."

"Are they for sale or aren't they?" Buck asked. His kind eyes twinkled with mirth. There would be no use in haggling with Buck Bryant—that much was obvious. Still, she had to try.

"Well, I actually brought them over for Grandma… who I never let pay for ornaments," Cozy began to explain. "So in truth, you can have them. I don't like accepting money from friends. It makes me uncomfortable and—"

"Well, I'd rather pay my friends for something than give the money to a complete stranger," Buck chuckled. "So…ten dollars apiece? Is that right?"

"Oh, no!" Cozy said, shaking her head as Buck retrieved his wallet from the back pocket of his jeans. "No, no, no. I won't take it…and I won't let you have the ornaments if you—"

"There," Buck said, pulling a hundred-dollar bill

out of his wallet and tossing it on the table.

"Mr. Bryant, really—"

"I spend three times that much on cookies from the little girls in my neighborhood every spring," he interrupted. "And these ornaments won't put ten pounds on my stomach. Besides, my sisters love little things like this. Furthermore, I know they don't own Cozy Robbins ornaments yet. They're hard to buy gifts for because we're all getting so old we have everything already." He reached out, taking hold of Cozy's hand. "You're doing me a favor, sweetheart. Really. Would you rather see an old man like me hobbling around at the mall, fighting the crowds in search of gifts for his sisters? Or would you rather just empty out your basket and save me the trouble?"

Cozy smiled at him. She wondered how anyone could keep from smiling at him. He was a real charmer. No wonder her grandma was gazing at him like a lovesick puppy.

"I highly doubt that you have ever hobbled, Mr. Bryant," Cozy said, relenting at last.

Buck smiled. "So I win?"

"Yes. You win," she sighed.

"Ahhh!" he said, rubbing his hands together with triumph. "Dottie, do you have a bag I can put these in?"

"You bet," Dottie said.

"I should wring your neck, Grandma," Cozy said as she began putting the ornaments back into their boxes.

Dottie simply shrugged and then retrieved a plastic

grocery sack from the cabinet under the sink.

There was a knock on the front door, and Dottie asked, "Would you mind letting Jesse in, Cozy? He refuses to just let himself in for some reason."

"That's because I taught him good manners," Buck explained.

"Okay," Cozy said, heading for the door.

"Here you go, Buck," she heard her grandmother say. "And I'll get some cider for Jesse."

Cozy opened the front door to see Jesse wiping his boots on the welcome rug and unfastening his tool belt. "So you're finished?" she asked, leaning to one side in an effort to look at the icicle lights hanging from the porch.

"Oh, no, you don't," he said, covering her face with one hand. "No peeking...not until it's dark."

Cozy was startled by the goose bumps racing over her as his hand lingered on her face a moment. She knew it was because his hand was cold, of course—but the goose bumps tickled all the same. She heard him drop his tool belt to the porch. In an instant, he had stepped into the house, closing the door behind him.

"I can't believe you were trying to peek," he teasingly scolded as he dropped his hand from her face. She could still feel the lingering sense of his fingers on her forehead and his thumb on her chin. The goose bumps hadn't subsided either.

"I didn't know I wasn't supposed to," she playfully defended herself.

"Come on in and have some cider, Jesse," Dottie

called from the kitchen. "It'll warm you right up!"

"Thanks," Jesse called in response. He smiled at Cozy. Taking hold of her arm, he pulled her with him toward the kitchen. "Come on. I don't trust you not to peek," he explained.

"I promise not to," she giggled as her goose bumps were renewed.

"Better safe than sorry," he said. "I take decorative illumination very seriously."

"I guess so," Cozy said as the sound of his chuckle caused butterflies to swarm in her stomach.

"Was she trying look?" Buck asked his grandson.

"Yep," Jesse answered.

"She's a stinker, Jess," Buck chuckled. "She's leaving my money on the table here, thinking she can walk out of here without it and that I'll take it back then."

Cozy started to argue, but she knew when she was caught.

"She's a stinker, all right," Dottie said, winking at her. "Now, Jesse, you sit down and have some cider with us. You've got to be chilled to the bone." Dottie set a mug of steaming mulled cider on the table next to Buck and another one next to hers. "Here you go, Cozy. I know you can't get enough of my cider."

Jesse's grip on Cozy's arms tightened a bit, causing her to look up at him. "No peeking," he said, his dazzling smile causing Cozy to feel a little dizzy and lightheaded. "Promise?"

"I promise," she sighed, rolling her eyes with exasperation.

"All right then." Still smiling, he nodded to Dottie as he sat down. "Thank you, Mrs. Robbins."

"Thank you, sweetie," Dottie said with a wink. "It's going to be so wonderful having lights up again...so festive."

"I've got all those grouchy old great-aunts of yours taken care of for Christmas," Buck said, picking up his own mug of cider and sipping from it.

"With these?" Jesse asked, reaching out to pick up one of the walnut ornaments Cozy hadn't yet put back in its box.

Cozy felt a blush rise to her cheeks as Jesse opened the hinged ornament, his eyes narrowing as he studied the tiny little nativity scene inside.

He looked to her, frowning. "You really made these?"

"Yeah," she managed to respond.

"These are awesome!" he mumbled, looking at the scene more intently. "Seriously...who would have the patience to do this?"

"Cozy Robbins would," Dottie answered, handing Jesse one of the white ornament boxes and pointing to the logo on the lid.

Jesse smiled. "Cozy Robbins," he said. "Now that's clever."

"Thank you," Dottie giggled. "It was my idea."

"Yes, it was," Cozy confirmed. At least she didn't have to be embarrassed about her ornaments and the origin of the logo.

"Cozy Robbins," Jesse repeated, still obviously

amused. He sipped at his cider. "Cozy Robbins. Cute. Awesome trade name and logo too." He closed the ornament and placed it in the box Dottie had provided. "Do you have any more?"

"Oh, no!" Cozy exclaimed. "I am not falling for that."

"Falling for what?" Jesse asked, though the innocent expression he tried to keep on his face simply screamed he was playing dumb. "Guys like Christmas. Maybe I want a few for my tree this year."

"And maybe I asked Santa for a pair of army boots," Cozy said.

Jesse nodded. "Those are good boots. I actually own several pair."

"Me too," Buck added, winking at Cozy.

"Oh, don't mind her, Jesse," Dottie interjected. "Cozy always keeps four or five extra ornaments in the trunk of her car this time of year...just in case somebody asks."

"Grandma!" Cozy scolded.

Buck and Jesse both chuckled into their mugs.

"So? How about it?" Jesse asked.

She could see he wasn't going to let it go any time soon. "Fine," Cozy relented. "I have five more in the car. You're welcome to them." She looked at him, her eyebrows arched in doubt. "You can have them for your *tree.*"

"Cool. How much?"

Just as Cozy started to say, "No cost," Buck piped in, "Fifty bucks for the five of them."

"Perfect," Jesse said, setting his mug down and reaching for his wallet.

"No. No, really. Please," Cozy pleaded. "L-let me just give them to you...as my thanks for doing Grandma's lights."

Jesse paused for a moment, frowned, and was thoughtful. "No. I don't like that," he said, shaking his head. Cozy sighed as he opened his wallet and withdrew a fifty-dollar bill. He tossed it on the table next to his grandfather's one-hundred-dollar bill and then picked up his mug again. "This is the best cider I've ever had, Mrs. Robbins."

"Well, thank you, sweetie," Dottie cooed. "It does a nice job of warming away a chill too." She looked to Cozy, saying, "Take a sip, Cozy. It'll settle you down a bit."

"I'm plenty settled, Grandma," Cozy said, rather plopping into her chair.

The cider was soothing, however, and she began to feel better.

"The sun should be down in half an hour or so," Jesse said. "Then we'll flip the switch and see if you approve of what I've done. I didn't do much, I'm afraid. I was running out of daylight and wanted to finish."

"I'm sure it will be beautiful, Jesse," Dottie assured him.

"We'll see."

Buck exhaled a slow sigh of contentment, and Cozy smiled at him. He was the sort of man that simply exuded old-fashioned charm, and she found herself again hoping something would spark between him and her grandmother.

"This is the life, isn't it, Jesse?" Buck asked. "Sitting in a cozy kitchen, sipping cider with two beautiful young ladies?"

Jesse smiled as Dottie blushed. "Yep. It doesn't get any better than this," he sighed.

Cozy stared at him over the rim of her mug as she sipped her cider. He was so handsome! He was certainly the handsomest man she'd ever seen. She almost giggled as the opening line to a playground song she and her friends used to sing in elementary school jingled through her mind—a song about sipping cider through a straw with the cutest boy a girl ever saw. Naturally, the song ended with the straw slipping so that the boy and the girl kissed. Cozy smiled as she continued to watch Jesse talk with her grandmother. She'd certainly like to sip cider through a straw with him!

Cozy shook her head and set her mug down on the table, disgusted with her adolescent daydreams. She needed a distraction—to get her mind off the goose bumps that had riddled her limbs when she'd thought about kissing Jesse. He was a complete stranger, for crying out loud!

"Put that money in your pocket before you forget, angel," Dottie suggested.

With a delicious smirk of triumph, Jesse picked the hundred and fifty dollars up off the table and handed it to Cozy. "Yeah. You don't want to forget this," he teased.

Rolling her eyes with exasperation, Cozy accepted the money and shoved it into the front pocket of her jeans. "Do you really put up a Christmas tree?" she asked him.

"Of course," he said. He returned to sipping his cider.

Cozy frowned a little, for she couldn't tell whether he was lying.

❧

The sun did finally set, and Cozy watched with amusement as Buck opened the front door for her grandmother, motioning for her to precede him in stepping out onto the porch.

"Oh, I'm so excited!" Dottie exclaimed.

"Cozy?" Buck nodded to Cozy, indicating she should precede him as well.

"Thank you," Cozy said as she stepped out onto the porch. Instantly, she wished she'd taken a moment to put her coat on. The evening air was already chilled.

"I hope you're not disappointed, Mrs. Robbins," Jesse said, closing the door behind them.

"Oh, sweetie! How could I be disappointed?" Dottie chirped. "One Christmas light on the house would be more than I've had in years. Though I do feel badly for taking up your day…your time and your strength."

"I like being outside," Jesse said. "And I know how ladies like their Christmas lights."

Cozy smiled as she saw Jesse wink at her grandmother. It really was a very kind gesture. She kept thinking that he must have an ulterior motive—that it couldn't possibly be he was just offering a random act of kindness. Still, she couldn't think of another reason, so she let it go—for the moment.

"Now, you all get out there to the sidewalk in front of the house," Jesse instructed. "And when you're ready, I'll turn them on for you."

"All right, son," Buck said. "Come on, Dottie. And watch yourself going down the stairs. It's pretty dark out tonight."

Cozy glanced to Jesse before following Buck and her grandmother out to the street. He grinned and nodded his assurance that she should go.

"Tell me when you guys are ready," he said.

"Okay," she agreed. She felt warm and delighted when he winked at her.

Hurrying after her grandmother and Buck, Cozy turned to face the house once she reached the sidewalk.

"Are you ready, Grandma?" she asked.

"Oh, yes! I can hardly stand it," Dottie chimed.

"We're ready!" Cozy called to Jesse.

Cozy gasped and her grandmother squealed with delight as the lights on the house suddenly shone forth through the dark. It was beautiful—simply beautiful! White icicle lights dripped from the eaves of both the upper and lower stories of her grandmother's home. Cozy had certainly seen icicle lights before, but these were different. They looked like actual icicles! She didn't know how Jesse had done it, but the icicle lights hung in varying lengths—some very long, some short, and some medium in length. The effect was overwhelming, appearing as if real icicles had formed on the eaves. It was so simplistic in design that it was far more enchanting than most icicle lights Cozy had seen on other houses.

"Oh, it's beautiful!" Dottie exclaimed. "It's the most beautiful thing I've ever seen. And look at the deer. Wherever did he get those deer anyway?"

Cozy wondered the same thing as she gazed on the lovely scene Jesse had fashioned on her grandmother's front lawn. Jesse had shaped strings of blue mini lights into a small waterfall that cascaded over a hedge and to then swirl into a pond. Three gold animated deer—illuminated with white lights—were positioned near the pond. A buck with a large set of antlers was poised in a majestic stance, slowly looking from side to side. A doe and fawn gradually lowered their heads to drink from the pond and then raised them once more. Two white swans—also illuminated with white lights—appeared to be floating gently on the opposite edge of the pond from the family of deer.

Cozy shook her head, awed by the display. It wasn't at all gaudy or overdone. It was perfect! And it was perfect for her grandma.

"Grandma!" she breathed. "It's so wonderful! I've never seen anything like it."

"Oh, I know," Dottie sighed. "It just takes my breath away."

"He does a good job, doesn't he?" Buck proudly asked.

"Oh, Buck! It's just...it's just perfect!" Dottie sighed.

Cozy smiled as she looked to her grandmother and saw the tears welling in her eyes.

"Well? Will it do for this year, Mrs. Robbins?" Jesse asked as he strode toward them.

"Will it do?" Dottie asked, brushing a tear from her cheek. "Oh, you dear, dear boy!" Throwing her arms around his neck, she hugged him—kissed him on the cheek. "It's so beautiful! Thank you so much. Oh, thank you so much!"

"You're welcome," Jesse chuckled. "As I said, I didn't have a whole lot of time left today, but I hope you'll enjoy it."

Dottie released him, brushing more tears from her eyes. "You're an angel, Jesse. Thank you so much. Now, how much do I owe you for the deer and lights and things?"

"Nothing. They're just some extra stuff I keep on hand in case I need them," Jesse said. "I'll just pack them up and take them all back home when the season is over."

"Are you sure?" Dottie asked.

"He's sure," Buck answered as Jesse nodded.

Cozy thought about the hundred and fifty dollars in her pocket. She felt sick about the fact that Jesse and his grandfather had insisted on paying for walnut ornaments when Jesse had gone to so much trouble for her grandmother's sake. Still, arguing the point with him would only upset her grandmother—spoil her joy in the beauty Jesse had created. Therefore, she bit her tongue and determined to sneak the money back to the men somehow.

"Do you have your car keys with you?" Jesse asked her.

"Yeah. Why?" she answered.

"I figure we can get my ornaments out of your trunk while we're already out here." He smiled with triumph, and Cozy sighed.

"Sure," she said, going to her car. She reached into her pocket and pushed the button on her key to pop the trunk. Quickly, she selected five white boxes out of the twenty she had in the trunk. She was glad she hadn't told Jesse how many she really had with her. She could only take so much charity.

Tossing them into one of the clear plastic bags she kept with them, she closed the trunk, returned to the sidewalk, and offered the bag to Jesse.

"You'll have to invite me over to see your Christmas tree when it's up," she baited him with a knowing smile.

"Okay," he agreed, however. He opened the plastic bag and peered in at the ornament boxes, even though the bag was transparent. "Did you pick out some good ones for me?"

"Of course," she assured him. She shivered then as the cold breeze nipped through her sweater.

"Let's get you ladies back inside before you freeze

to death," Buck said, taking Dottie's arm and linking it with his own.

"I could just stay out here all night looking at this," Dottie sighed, gazing at the house as she and Buck started up the walkway.

"You'd be an ice sculpture by morning, Grandma," Cozy giggled as she followed them.

"Do you think she really likes it?" Jesse quietly asked from behind her.

Cozy stopped cold, turned, and looked at him with disbelief. "Are you kidding? It's perfect! She's crying! How could you even wonder?"

Jesse shrugged, and she was astounded as she realized he truly wasn't certain he'd done a good enough job with the lights. "I don't know. I just like to make sure older people are pampered, you know?"

Cozy's heart fluttered along with the butterflies in her stomach, and she smiled at him. "Me too. And I promise you...this is more wonderful for her than you can even imagine. Thank you, Jesse."

"You're welcome," he said, grinning. "Now let's get inside before *you're* an ice sculpture."

They all sat in the family room for nearly two more hours. Dottie and Buck sat close together on the sofa before the fire, while Jesse and Cozy sat in opposing chairs on either side of it. It was a comfortable, friendly evening, and Cozy began to dread returning home to the chaos of her brothers and sisters finishing up last-minute homework. Still, as her grandma's cuckoo announced eight o'clock, Cozy sighed and stood up from her chair.

"I have to go, Grandma," she said. She went to the sofa and bent down, hugging her grandma tightly. "I'll come tomorrow after work though, and we can finish making the list of what you need for Thanksgiving. Okay?"

"Perfect!" Dottie answered. "Did I tell you that Buck has accepted my invitation to have him and Jesse join us for Thanksgiving dinner?"

"H-he did?" Cozy stammered. She glanced to Jesse, who smiled and shrugged his shoulders as if it was the first time he'd heard of it too.

"Yes...and I'm so excited about everyone being together," Dottie cooed.

"Well, that's awesome!" Cozy giggled. "Maybe you can bake an extra pie just for Jesse, Grandma...as thanks for all his hard work today."

Dottie gasped with delight. "Yes, I'll do that!" She looked to Jesse and asked, "You do like pumpkin pie, don't you, Jesse?"

"Of course, ma'am," he said, smiling. "But I don't want you to go to any extra trouble."

"Oh, it's no trouble at all! I'd love to do something for you in return."

"Well, enjoy your ornaments, boys," Cozy said, looking to Mr. Bryant and then to Jesse. She arched one eyebrow as her attention lingered on the handsome man sitting in a nearby chair. "And I'll be interested to see that Christmas tree of yours, Jesse."

He chuckled. "I'm sure you will."

"Now don't forget to take that box of extra crackle glass I picked up today, Cozy," Dottie instructed.

"I won't," Cozy said. "Good night, everyone."

"Goodnight, Cozy," Mr. Bryant said as Jesse rose from his chair and started toward her.

"Let me help you with your stuff," he said.

"Oh, it's okay. It's just one box and a basket. I can manage," she assured him. But he didn't stop—just strode past her into the entryway.

Cozy was surprised when he took her red coat down from the coat hook by the front door. "Here you go," he said.

"Thank you." Cozy felt herself blush, for as she reached out for her coat, he simply held it up, indicating he meant to assist her in putting it on. In her entire life, a man had never offered to help her on with her coat. Well, sure, her father—but only when she was little enough to need help. Nervously, she slipped one arm into one sleeve and then the other into the other, muttering, "Thank you," when he'd finished helping her. She was further astonished when Jesse then opened the front door for her, nodding as a gesture she should exit through it.

"I'll carry your stuff to your car for you," he said, bending down to pick up the box containing the rest of the crackle glass and her basket her grandmother had set by the front door for her.

"Oh, you don't have to—" she began.

"I don't have to do anything," he said. "It's my

pleasure." He grinned at her, and her heart began to pound like a hammer on an anvil. His smile was purely big-screen movie-star quality! It dazzled her to near dumbfoundedness for a moment.

"After you," he said.

Cozy stepped out onto the porch, and Jesse closed the door behind them. As she started down the walkway toward the street, she bit her lip to stifle the delighted giggle that bubbled up in her throat when she heard him whistling—whistling the melody to the old Sam the Sham and the Pharaohs song "Li'l Red Riding Hood" as he followed her down the walkway toward the street.

She couldn't help but glance back at him with a smile, and he winked as he continued to whistle. "Very funny," she giggled.

"Do you want this in the trunk?" he asked as they approached her car.

"Sure," she said, pressing the button on her car key to pop the trunk.

Jesse continued to whistle as he opened the trunk and set the box inside. He closed the hatch and walked to the driver's side door of the car. Still whistling the song, he nodded to her to indicate she should push the button to unlock her door. He couldn't be serious. Did he really mean to open the car door for her? It was an archaic gesture—and entirely fabulous.

Cozy pushed the button and heard the door unlock. Jesse then opened the car door and motioned for her to get in.

"Thank you," she said, sliding into the driver's seat of her car.

"My pleasure," Jesse said. "Now, you have yourself a good evening, Little Red Riding Hood," he chuckled. "And watch out for those wolves." He winked at her, and she heard a growl (sounding very much like that of a wolf) rumble low in his throat as he closed the car door. He began to whistle the tune again as he nodded at her through the window, before turning and starting back toward the house.

Every inch of Cozy's flesh was alive with a thrilling tingling sensation. She was breathless—totally breathless. How could it be that he'd managed to render her so awash with pleasure with such a simple teasing? With a trembling hand, she turned the key in the ignition, and the engine roared to life.

Jesse watched Cozy drive away. "Hmm," he hummed to himself. Miss Cozy Robbins didn't seem to realize how alluring she was. He liked that about her. He wondered for a moment if it would be terribly inappropriate to pursue the girl who he rather hoped would end up being his grandpa's step-granddaughter. He smiled, amused as he considered the rather wolfish attraction he felt toward her.

"Ow-ooo," he howled quietly. He chuckled and returned to whistling "Li'l Red Riding Hood" as he opened the door to Mrs. Robbins's house and stepped inside.

CHAPTER FIVE

Thanksgiving Day dawned bright and beautiful. If nothing else, Cozy was thankful she didn't have to work at the café for two days. The new male customer who had started dining in for lunch every day was far too vulgar and forward, and Cozy was thankful she wouldn't have to deal with him for once.

And yet there were many other more wonderful things Cozy was thankful for. She was thankful for her family, her grandmother, the fact that she even had a job. She was thankful that her ornament sales were over and that she'd made enough to pay her tuition in January. However, there was a new something she was thankful for. As Cozy stood next to her grandmother in her grandmother's kitchen, sautéing the vegetables for the stuffing as her grandma crumbled the cornbread, she was silently thanking the heavens for Jesse Bryant.

She'd seen him nearly every evening since the day he put up her grandma's Christmas lights the week before. And every day that she'd seen him, she'd grown more and more fond of him. He was thoughtful, witty, and very masculine. Since the day he'd leapt off the roof to help the little boy across the street free his head from the iron fence bars, Jesse had continued to prove purely heroic. All the Christmas lights he'd put up aside, he'd pushed an older lady's car down the street to the gas station when she'd run out of gas nearby. He'd replaced some missing shingles on his grandfather's roof. When he'd been chopping more firewood for his grandfather, he filled her grandmother's woodbin as well. There were several other things Cozy had witnessed that demonstrated Jesse Bryant's capability and good character, as well. Therefore, just knowing him—just being in his company and being the recipient of his dazzling smile—inspired thoughts of gratitude and delight in Cozy.

Naturally, she didn't tell anyone about Jesse, other than Mindy, and even then she didn't share much. She liked keeping him a secret. She liked to pretend that no other woman in the world knew him—only her. Somehow the pretense had allowed her to be more comfortable in his company, and she had become quite comfortable with him. Cozy loved the way Jesse made her feel—pretty, witty, and interesting. He always chuckled or laughed at her silly puns—always encouraged her toward confidence. Furthermore, she simply loved the way he'd wink at her, softly growl, and start whistling "Li'l Red Riding Hood" whenever he saw her in her red hooded coat. Cozy determined she'd never own another coat she liked more—not in all her life, even if she lived to be a hundred.

Yes, Jesse Bryant was something to be thankful

for. Oh, Cozy knew he was probably just interested in nurturing the growing friendship between his grandfather and her grandmother—that she was just a byproduct of it. Still, she enjoyed his company. More than enjoyed it—savored and craved it.

Thus, as she stirred the sautéing vegetables in the skillet, she smiled—for what woman wouldn't smile at the thought of Jesse Bryant? As goose bumps broke over her arms at the lingering thoughts of him, Cozy tried to avert the musings of her mind. She glanced to her grandma—her rosy-cheeked, Christmas-carol-humming grandma.

Dottie Robbins has been on cloud nine since the day Buck Bryant moved in next door. Cozy thought that if there were only nine clouds in the sky—the ninth being the highest and closest to heaven—then her grandmother was skipping around on top of it. Cozy hadn't seen her grandmother that happy since before her grandfather had passed away. Sometimes, late at night, Cozy would worry about what would happen if Mr. Bryant's interest turned from her grandmother. But each time doubt would enter her mind, she would simply push it away. Still, she kept hoping for a moment alone with Jesse somehow—a moment that would give her the opportunity to ask him about his grandfather's true feelings toward her grandmother. Did Buck like Dottie better than he liked most women—or at least differently than he liked most women? Buck's treatment of Cozy's grandmother led her to believe that he did favor her. Yet Buck was like Jesse—considerate to everyone, friendly and helpful to anybody.

Turning down the burner flame under the skillet, Cozy hoped that she would have a chance to talk to Jesse about it sometime during the day. With everyone that was coming to her grandma's house for Thanksgiving dinner, surely she would be able to pull him aside for a moment.

"Did I tell you that I invited that nice Brittany and her little boy, Tyler, to have dinner with us today?" Dottie asked.

"What?" Cozy gasped, frowning. "Why?"

Dottie's face scrunched into an expression of confusion. "I thought you'd want me to. She's alone, you know, with her recent divorce and everything, and I thought Tyler might have fun with Carol's kids. They're all so close to his age, and I'm sure he needs some friends and playtime." She frowned. "I really thought you'd be glad I invited them."

"Oh...oh, I am," Cozy fibbed. "It's just that... well...it's just that..."

Dottie smiled with sudden understanding. "Don't worry, sweet pea. You've got Jesse Bryant eating out of the palm of your hand. Believe me...he's not going to give poor little Brittany the time of day."

Cozy blushed, mortified that her grandma had read her so easily. "I *wish* I had him eating out of the palm of my hand," she confessed in a whisper.

"Honey," her grandma began, lowering her voice as if conspiring, "if I wiped rubber cement on your palm, Jesse Bryant would eat it. He'd lick it right off!"

Cozy laughed. "Rubber cement, Grandma? You're so funny!" She shook her head, entirely amused and feeling much better about Brittany and her son attending the dinner. After all, her grandma was right. They were alone and needed friendship and support. Though she did not believe for one second that Jesse Bryant would eat rubber cement or anything else out of her hand, she did feel better—a little.

"I understand, sweetie," Dottie said. "Vicki Murray is coming today too. And I know the second she lays eyes on Buck…well, I'll be lucky to get a word in the rest of the day."

"Vicki?" Cozy whined. "Oh, Grandma. She drives you crazy!"

Dottie shrugged. "I know. But she doesn't have any family nearby, and no one offered to have her. So…I did."

"Well, Buck Bryant really does eat out of your palm, Grams," Cozy assured her. "He's over here every evening. Do you really think your mulled cider is *that* good?"

Dottie smiled and then shrugged again. "I don't know. I worry that I should be a little more mature and a little less like a high school girl when it comes to my feelings toward him. But I can't help it! He just gives me the worst butterflies in my stomach. It's awful!"

"It's wonderful!" Cozy giggled. "And he likes you. I can tell by the way he looks at you."

"That's just because his eyes are blue. People with

101

blue eyes always give you the sensation that they're looking right into your soul."

"Oh, it's not that," Cozy argued, however. "He smiles too. He can't keep from smiling at you. That's proof that he thinks you're hot."

Dottie laughed. "Oh, yes...I'm sure that's it. He thinks I'm hot. After all, I'm so sexy these days with all my wrinkles and age spots and things."

"You are, Grandma," Cozy assured her. "I'm going to watch him today...because I'm sure I caught him looking at your bum the other night."

"Cozy Robbins!" Dottie exclaimed. "What a thing to say!"

Cozy could see the delight on her grandma's face, however. "It's true. I saw him."

"Hello? Mom?" It was Cozy's Aunt Carol calling from the entryway.

"We're in here, dear," Dottie called.

A moment later, three children came bounding into the kitchen. "Hi, Grandma!" Cozy's eight-year-old cousin Andrew greeted. He threw his arms around Dottie's waist and hugged her tight.

"Well, hello, sweetie," Dottie said, returning his hug and kissing him on the top of his little blonde head.

"Hi, Grandma! We're here!" Kimberly and Lisa chimed as they skipped into the kitchen.

"Hi, Cozy!" Kimberly said, hugging Cozy first.

"Hi, Kimberly," Cozy giggled. "Are you excited for Thanksgiving?"

"I am!" the six-year-old giggled. "Especially the pie!"

"Me too! Me too!" Lisa pouted. "I'm as excited as Kimberly is, Cozy."

"I know you are, Lisa," Cozy said, hugging her five-year-old cousin.

Cozy smiled and sighed. The serenity was over. Soon her own brothers and sisters would arrive, and Aunt Carol's husband, Ethan (whose booming voice would begin reverberating through the house like a thunderstorm). Still, Jesse and his grandpa would arrive too—and even though she might never have the chance to talk to Jesse all the day long, she could look at him. That in itself was something to look forward to. She wondered if having children and teenagers bouncing off the wall all day would scare either Mr. Bryant or Jesse away. She hoped not.

Thanksgiving dinner with family, neighbors, and friends came and went in the usual flurry of chaos. It was an enjoyable meal, but Cozy wondered how anyone managed to get through it without a serious case of indigestion. Furthermore, several things Cozy had fearfully predicted did, in fact, transpire. First and foremost was the fact that Brittany Jackman talked a blue streak to Jesse any time the opportunity presented itself. Though Cozy felt hot with jealousy and irritated with the entire situation, she noted that, although Jesse was kind to Brittany, he was in no way smitten with her flattering and attention. It helped soothe her anxieties a little.

She could also see the worry and anxiety sloshing around in her grandmother as she watched Vicki Murray shamelessly flirt with Buck. However, Cozy noted the way Buck would wink at her grandmother across the table, smile at her, and brush her arm with his as often as he could. Dottie was safe. Buck obviously liked her grandmother—no matter how hard Vicki Murray tried to own his attention.

Once the meal was over, Dottie insisted that everyone just relax and have fun. Cozy had always admired the way her grandma put people and visiting before dishes and cleanup. Dottie's way of thinking was that there would always be dishes to do, but there wouldn't always be time to visit with family and friends. Therefore, as everyone else began to settle in the family room or linger around the dinner table in talking, Cozy went with Lisa and Kimberly to pull out the plastic storage bins that were lovingly referred to as "Grandma's toys."

Soon, Andrew and his sisters, Tyler Jackman, and Cozy's young brothers were in the den at the back of the house playing with plastic farm and zoo animals, building blocks, and little timber logs. When Cozy returned to the family room after retrieving the toys to find Brittany chattering away with Jesse, however, she couldn't face not having his attention. She knew it was shallow—adolescently jealous and immature—but she couldn't help it. So she returned to the dining room and sat down at the table, where her father and her Uncle Ethan were discussing the best ways to winterize a house.

After twenty minutes of listening about what the best way was to blow out a sprinkler system and which brand of storm windows was most heat-conservative, Cozy made her excuses and left the dining room. She needed some air—and some peace and quiet.

Retrieving her coat from the hallway closet, she started toward the backdoor. She paused, however, when she heard Jesse's voice coming from the den.

"Look...see there?" he was saying. "Now you have a zoo. See, all these fences and corrals are where you guys can set up your different animal exhibits. Look, this is your tiger habitat."

Heading for the den, Cozy smiled when she peeked in to see Jesse lounging on the floor next to a vast fencing system built of little timber logs. It was obvious he'd helped the children really make a fine project out of their toys, and the knowledge caused her heart to swell.

"That's awesome, Jesse!" Andrew exclaimed.

"Yeah," Jesse agreed. "Now, decide where you want to put your animal exhibits, and then you can use these dollhouse dolls as the zoo guests, and you guys can all have fun together...girls and boys. Okay?"

It was then that Cozy noticed Kimberly and Lisa sitting to one side with frowns and pouty lips.

"Okay...I guess," Kimberly mumbled.

Jesse looked up then, catching sight of Cozy.

"Are you going outside?" he asked.

Cozy smiled as she nodded to him, for he suddenly looked desperate for escape.

"Do you wanna take a walk with me?" he asked, hopping to his feet before she even had a chance to respond.

"Sure," she giggled as he grabbed his coat off the back of a nearby chair and hurried toward her.

"We wanna come!" Lisa whined.

"Oh, you don't want to miss out on the zoo fun, do you, baby?" Jesse asked, taking hold of Cozy's arm and turning her toward the backdoor. "And besides...it's cold out there. We don't want you getting the sniffles, now do we?"

Jesse didn't wait for a response—simply led Cozy toward the backdoor and liberation.

"Ahh!" he sighed once they were outside.

Cozy giggled. "A little too overwhelming in there for you, Mr. Bryant?" she teased.

He smiled at her. "Maybe a little. Nothing some fresh air and a walk won't fix." He studied her a moment. "A little too overwhelming in there for *you*, Miss Robbins?"

"Nothing some fresh air and a walk won't fix," she admitted.

"Then let's go," he said, nodding toward the path that led to the front of the house.

Cozy nodded, and they started out.

Once they reached the sidewalk, she was delighted when Jesse stepped around behind her, moving to walk between her and the street. It was a very gentlemanly gesture and made her stomach do a flip-flop.

"The leaves are so pretty this year," Cozy noted aloud as they walked beneath a canopy of gold.

"They are," he agreed. "And they've hung on longer than usual."

"Yeah. It's been a pretty mild autumn so far…but I'm sure the winds will start soon and take them all away from me."

She heard him chuckle and turned to look up at him. He was smiling at her, as if she'd said something that pleased him.

"I like the way you put that," he said. "Like the wind is some bad guy, stealing away your treasure."

Cozy giggled and shrugged. "I guess I kind of do feel that way about it, now that you mention it."

"I know what you mean," he said. "I enjoy the holidays, especially Christmas, but I don't really like winter too much."

"I would live in perpetual fall if I could," Cozy sighed. "I like summer too, but winter and spring… they're just kind of not fun."

"Today is nice though," he said. He exhaled a heavy sigh.

They were both quiet then. The breeze rippled the dry leaves beneath their feet—tickled the gold ones overhead. The scent of neighborhood fireplace smoke lingered in the air, warm and soothing. Cozy sighed as the noise and chaos sailing through her grandmother's house rinsed away.

"Can I ask you something?" Jesse ventured.

"Sure," Cozy answered.

"What do you think about my grandpa and your grandma?"

Cozy smiled. "What do you mean what do I think?"

He shrugged broad shoulders—shoulders Cozy suddenly had the desire to lay her head against. "You know...would you mind if things...developed between them? Went to a different level?"

"You mean like if they started dating or something?" she asked. She was delighted to know that he'd been thinking over similar things that she had where their grandparents were concerned.

"Yeah. Or even, you know...if they...you know..." he stammered.

She giggled, for his discomfort was wildly endearing. "If they fell in love and maybe got married?"

"Yeah," he confirmed. She bit her lip to keep from giggling again, for he seemed relieved that she had said what he was thinking so he didn't have to. "Would you be okay with it?"

"Of course!" she exclaimed. "If you want to know a secret...I'm hoping that's what happens."

"Me too," he admitted, smiling with relief. "So then, are you up for helping me to move things along between them?"

Cozy was still amused—and very intrigued. Yet she was curious as well.

"How do you mean?" she inquired. "Aren't they

already spending every evening together at Grandma's house?"

He chuckled. "Yeah. Grandpa's been drinking so much cider that he swears it's totally messed up his bladder."

Cozy laughed. "Really?"

"Yep. Men can usually go almost all day without one visit to the bathroom. But Grandpa says he's up all night now. He says your grandma sure loves for him to drink her cider."

Cozy laughed again. "Oh, she loves for everyone to drink her cider," she explained. "She's very proud of how good it is. And I think she also associates people's happiness and contentment with it. As if her cider makes everything all right."

Jesse laughed. "It kind of does, though...doesn't it?"

Cozy nodded. "Yeah, I guess it does."

"Anyway, I was thinking that if we gave them more time alone...you know?" he continued. "We're always over there with them...because they seem to want us there, right?"

"You're right. They do," Cozy said, only just then realizing the fact.

"Well, what if we just start, you know, easing into the other rooms or something," he suggested. "You know what I mean? We can leave them in the kitchen to their cider and ruining my grandpa's bladder... and you and I can just hang out in the front room or something. I think they need that."

"Yeah. I do too."

"I mean, we can't be too obvious about it, or they'll wise up to what we're trying to do," he said. "But I know there're things I wouldn't say to a woman if there were other people listening."

"Really? Like what?" she asked. She understood exactly what he meant, but she was curious as to what he would actually say to a woman he was alone with.

He shrugged. "I don't know. Just, like, confessions of how I really felt and stuff like that. I know Grandpa has it bad for your grandma…but he's not going to tell her with you and me sitting right there listening."

Cozy couldn't help but smile. The delight rising in her for her grandma's sake was wonderful.

"Does he really like her that much, do you think?" she asked. "I mean, she feels like she likes him more than he likes her."

"Oh, no, he's completely freaked out over her," he confirmed. "It's kind of funny to watch. When he talks about her, he gets all mushy, and his eyes kind of glaze over. It's intense."

"Well, good…'cause she sounds like she's sixteen years old when she talks about him."

"Let's get them together then," he suggested. "We'll continue to chaperone—because for some reason they want us there with them—but we'll just be more stealth. You know?"

"Okay," Cozy said. "It's funny. I was going to try and find a way to talk to you about it today too."

"You see? We think alike," he said, smiling. "At

least where Buck and Dottie's budding romance is concerned."

"Budding romance?" Cozy giggled.

"Yeah. Isn't that what you girls call it?" he teased.

"I guess we do think alike," she admitted.

"What else do you think?" he inquired.

"About what?"

"About anything."

Cozy thought for a moment. "Hmm. Too nonspecific. You have to offer me a subject."

"Okay." He frowned and was quiet for a few seconds. "What do you think about kids?"

"Do you mean other people's kids?"

"Other people's kids and having ones of your own," he specified. "Answer honestly now."

"Okay...honestly...I love kids," she said. "But I know I'll like my kids more than I like other people's kids."

Jesse nodded with approval. He liked her answer—and he liked her honesty.

"So you want to have kids?" he asked next. "How many?"

Cozy shrugged. "At least three, but less than six. How about you?"

"I like kids too. But I agree that I'll like my kids more than I'll like other people's kids."

Jesse frowned a moment. Was he subconsciously fishing—trying to find out how Cozy Robbins felt about family for his own reasons? He'd already decided to pursue her—whether or not things worked out between his grandpa and her grandmother. But he didn't want to freak her out and scare her off either. Still, she answered honestly—hadn't seemed uncomfortable about the question.

"How many kids to *you* want?" she asked.

He smiled. "More than one, less than five," he answered honestly.

She giggled and nodded her approval.

She looked so cute in her little red coat! Again he thought he was too much the wolf where his intentions toward her were concerned. But he couldn't help it.

"My turn," she said then. "Name the president of the United States that you think was the greatest."

"Wow! Politics," he chuckled. "Don't be shy, now, Little Red. Get right to the serious stuff."

"You asked about kids," she reminded him. "That's serious."

"I guess," he admitted. "Hmm. I can only choose one, right?"

"Right."

"Okay...and I realize I'm being very brave here... taking a chance that you might gouge my eyes out if I answer wrong," he began. He paused however.

"It's an opinion question," she giggled. "Not a life or death one."

"Okay then...at the risk of sounding cliché, I really would have to go with Abraham Lincoln," he said. "There. I've said it." He looked to her to see her smiling as if she had some secret delight. "And you're not running or gouging out my eyes."

"Nope," she said. "You just named my first choice too."

"Really?"

"Yep."

"Okay," he sighed. "My turn." He was pensive for a moment, trying to decide what he could ask her that would reveal something about her character he wanted to know. He already knew she was beautiful, kind, family-oriented, and smart. But there was more he wanted to know. In truth, he wanted to know everything about her. In truth, he hoped that someday he would.

"Your feelings on premarital…um…*intimacy*…are?"

Cozy nearly passed out! Had he really asked her what she thought about sex before marriage? Or had she misunderstood?

"D-do you mean intimacy as in kissing, cuddling, hugging?" she ventured.

"Intimacy as in the ultimate intimacy between a man and a woman," Jesse clarified.

Cozy was trembling. "And you thought I was brazen for bringing up politics?"

"Come on. Be brave, Little Red," he urged her. "I'm not going to eat you because of your answer."

"But will you still walk home with me no matter what my answer is?" she asked.

He chuckled. "Of course."

Cozy still paused a moment. She knew very well that most men would think her answer was wrong—that most men would dub her a *prude* for it. Yet she had to take the risk. And besides, she knew Jesse's reaction to her answer would be very telling.

"I-I think the ultimate intimacy between a man and a woman, as you call it, should only take place after marriage…with the person you're married to, of course." There! She'd said it, and the chips would have to fall where they would.

"Agreed," he said as if the question had been the most trivial in the world. "So…I'm guessing your grandma feels the same way?"

Cozy was simultaneously relieved that Jesse held to a high moral standard and disappointed that he hadn't been asking her the question because he wanted to know where she stood on the issue but rather because he wanted to know where her grandmother stood.

"Of course," she answered a little too tersely.

"Good. Grandpa's that way too," he said. "I just wanted to be sure it was safe to leave those two kids alone in the house together." He winked at her, and it softened her indignation a little.

"Okay, your turn," he prodded.

"I'm at a loss for words," she admitted. "You trumped me on the bold question meter."

He laughed. "Okay. I'll let you off the hook."

"Do you have to work tomorrow?" she asked him. She wasn't even sure why she asked, but the question had just popped into her head as a change of subject.

"Yeah," he answered. "We got a big decorating job downtown, and I think my crew will need the extra help if they're going to get it finished in time."

"I didn't know electricians were so into decorating for Christmas," she teased.

He shrugged. "It's a job site with a paycheck attached. It could be worse."

Cozy smiled. She liked that he did Christmas lights. She liked that he was willing to work alongside the men in his crew.

"What about you?" he began. "Are you a Black Friday shopper?"

Cozy shook her head. "I'm finished with my Christmas gifts and shopping. I'm a Black Friday gift wrapper. Every year Grandma and I get together and wrap. We put on the Christmas music, drag the pretty wrapping stuff out of the garage—"

"Drink mulled cider..." he interjected.

Cozy giggled, "Exactly. It's one of my favorite days of the year. I absolutely avoid the mall and stuff if I can possibly help it." She glanced to him. "How about you? Do you have gifts to get for people?"

"A couple...but I make most of mine."

"You make them? You mean like...arts and crafts? Like those little key chains braided out of leather strips boys make at scout camps and stuff?"

"No," he answered, smiling. "Though I do know how to make those."

"Why am I not surprised?" she teased.

"No. My gifts are homemade, but there's no glue,

tape, or strips of leather involved. Just sugar and dead animals."

"What?" Cozy asked, wrinkling her nose. "Are you, like, a taxidermist slash sugar beet farmer or something?"

"No. But that would be an interesting theme for, like, a serial killer movie or something." He chuckled. "No. I make my own beef jerky. That's where the dead animals come in." He winked at her.

"And the sugar?" she asked.

"Baby...my roasted raspberry almonds will change your life," he answered.

Just the fact that he'd called her *baby* was enough to send her heart pounding like a meat tenderizer. But the fact that he'd mention almond and raspberry in the same breath made her mouth water.

"Raspberry almonds?" she squeaked. He'd really thrown her for a loop with the *baby* thing.

"Yep. It's an old family recipe," he explained. Lowering his voice, he teased, "We're all very secretive about it."

"Oh, I see," she said, rolling her eyes.

"But seriously, me and Grandpa are the only ones who still know how to make them." His smile faded a bit. "My parents used to get us all together when we were kids, and we'd make them. We'd make hundreds of pounds of them...literally. Some of them we gave to friends and neighbors on Christmas Eve as gifts, and some of them we sold to other people who wanted them." He looked at her, his smile returning. "Kind of like your ornaments, you know?"

"It sounds like a lot of work," Cozy said.

"Yeah." He winked at her. "But making ornaments out of walnuts is unfathomable to me." His eyebrows suddenly arched as if inspiration had only just hit him. "Hey! We're like soul mates or something. We both do Christmas stuff that revolves around nuts."

Cozy laughed. He was too funny! "Yeah, I guess we do," she said. "So you still make these raspberry almonds every year?"

"Yeah. Me and Grandpa do it. They're awesome!" He looked at her and winked. "Seriously, you'll never be the same once you've tasted them. They change your life."

"I can't wait to try them then."

"They're delicious," he said. "You'd think I'd be tired of them after all these years...that they wouldn't be special. But they are. I suppose they remind me of my parents and the good old days before my brothers all decided money was more important than anything else. Either way, Grandpa and I are the only ones who still make them...but all three of my brothers still like to get them for Christmas."

"How do I get on the list?" Cozy asked. "You can't tempt me with something raspberry-flavored that will change my life and then deprive me of it. That's mean."

"Oh, believe me, Little Red Riding Hood," he chuckled, "there are several things this big bad wolf could tempt you with that would change your life."

117

Cozy gasped, simultaneously thrilled and astonished at his implication. "Well, I guess I walked right into that one," she said, shaking her head.

"You sure did," he confirmed. "But to answer your question, there's nothing you have to do to get on my list. You're already on it."

"Well, how much do I owe you then?" she asked as the word *payback* began to flash in her mind.

"Nothing. They'll be my Christmas gift to you and your grandma," he answered.

"So I'm expected to take your money for my goofy walnut ornaments, but you won't let me pay for your almonds?" she challenged.

"Apples and watermelons, Cozy Robbins," he said. "My almonds and jerky are my gifts to people. Your walnuts are your business. And besides, I really did want them for my tree, and we didn't know each other as well way back then."

"Way back then?" Cozy exclaimed in amused disbelief. "It was a week ago, Jesse Bryant."

He shrugged. "A week is a long time in certain situations."

"You're just squiggling out of it," she told him.

"Listen, Cozy," he began, "my raspberry walnuts... after you've tasted them, you'll forgive me for anything...even paying you for your ornaments."

"Oh, really?" she asked, smiling as he took hold of her arm to stop their walk and turned her to face them.

"After you've had my raspberry walnuts, you won't care whether I'm a wolf in sheep's clothing...or a taxidermist slash beet-farmer serial-killer. You'll be completely under my control."

"Wow!" she said with extra dramatics. "Those must be some raspberry almonds."

"You're damn right," he confirmed.

Cozy's eyebrows arched at the strength of his assurance. "Well, then...I can't wait to try them."

He smiled at her, and she nearly melted into a puddle of warm syrup at his feet. His expression was rather...well, rather wolfish—as if he were a sly predator and she his prey.

"There's a bench," he said then, pointing to a place behind her. "Do you wanna sit and watch the leaves for a while?"

"I'd love it," she answered—and she knew she would.

Time became irrelevant to Cozy as she sat on the bench with Jesse beneath a canopy of gold-leafed cottonwoods. They talked about seemingly everything under the sun—from what their favorite Italian foods were to the state of the national economy. They planned ways in which to create moments of privacy for their grandparents. They laughed over embarrassing experiences they'd each had—even told stupid jokes to one another.

And there was more. Cozy loved lingering in Jesse's presence—bathed in the unfamiliar bliss of it—the way his strong body emanated a masculine heat that warmed her as he sat next to her on the bench. She reveled in the way he'd lean back and stretch, resting his arms on the back of the bench with one positioned across her back. And every so often, as the autumn breezes would whisper through the trees, they'd pause—watching as leaves of bright yellow-gold drifted down from the branches overhead, the rustle of the leaves in the street and the sidewalk seeming to be the only sound in the world.

In fact, it wasn't until the sun began to set that Cozy even realized how long they'd been gone—hours! The Thanksgiving meal had ended at one p.m., and she knew the sun had been setting at about six in the evening. Surely they couldn't have been gone four hours!

"I suppose we should get back," Jesse said, as if he'd been reading her most recent thoughts. "Your grandma will think the wolf in me won out and I've devoured you or something."

"I should get back and start the dishes," Cozy sighed. "I'm sure they're piled to the ceiling by now."

"Come on then," Jesse said, standing and offering a hand to her to help her. "I'll help you so Grandpa and Dottie can have some time together."

Cozy smiled and placed her hand in his. She stood, disappointed that her time alone with Jesse was over.

"Thanks for coming with me," she said as they started back up the sidewalk.

"Thanks for rescuing me from playing zoo," he chuckled.

"Oh, you loved it," she teased him.

He shrugged. "It was okay...but I'm more of a little green plastic army men kind of guy."

"Well, all I know is, I can't wait for Christmas now," Cozy sighed. "You and your raspberry almonds. My mouth is watering."

"For me? Or the almonds?" he teased with a wink.

"You're so bad!" she scolded, playfully slapping his arm.

"Grrr," he growled, winking at her.

Cozy giggled when he began whistling "Li'l Red Riding Hood" as they walked home beneath an orange sunset autumn sky.

CHAPTER SIX

All through the next day, Cozy Robbins felt as if she were skipping along beside her grandmother on that old proverbial cloud nine. In truth, she was beside her grandmother all the next day—only they were reveling in wrapping Christmas gifts, drinking cider, and baking cookies together. Still, whenever Cozy even thought about Jesse Bryant, butterflies erupted in her stomach, and she couldn't help but smile.

Furthermore, her grandmother had explained early in the day that Buck had been very attentive to her after the dinner guests had all left. He'd been there when Jesse and Cozy returned from their walk, of course—which was much more than Cozy could say for anyone else. Everyone had left long before they had returned from their walk, including Cozy's family. She'd felt guilty for a moment too, at having not been there to say good-bye to her Aunt Carol, Uncle Ethan, and cousins. But her guilt hadn't lingered long, for the sheer pleasure of being isolated in Jesse's company for so long was worth the sacrifice of propriety. These emotions confused Cozy at first, for she wasn't one to neglect people's feelings. They were a little frightening too. For the first time in her life, Cozy had chosen someone else above her family and friends—Jesse. Moreover, she had consciously determined that she would do the same thing again if the opportunity arose. She liked him that much; she was that drawn to him.

Oh, she didn't harbor too many unrealistic fantasies where Jesse Bryant was concerned. After all, it was hard to believe that a man like him even existed—let alone that a man like Jesse would find Cozy interesting enough to really have any sort of serious relationship with.

Even so, her grandmother was encouraging—unknowingly, of course—but encouraging all the same. All the day long, Cozy's grandmother had spoken of her insecurities where Buck was concerned—her inability to believe she could really capture his heart.

"I mean, surely a man like Buckly Bryant could never see anything in me that would be so unique or special enough to waste too much time on. Not for any real length of time anyway," Dottie said as she handed Cozy a piece of transparent gift-wrap tape.

"Grandma," Cozy began, "believe me…Buck adores you. I know he does. Don't be such a doubtful chicken."

"Chicken?" Dottie exclaimed with playful indignation. "I sat closer to him on the couch last night than I ever have. How does that qualify me as a chicken?"

"You're right," Cozy admitted. "I guess what I was

really trying to say is...go for it! Don't be afraid to let him know how much you like him."

"Hmm," Dottie hummed. "Isn't that the pot calling the kettle black, sweet pea?"

"I don't know what you mean," Cozy said, playing ignorant.

"What did go on between you two yesterday, anyway?" Dottie asked. "You were gone for hours and hours."

Cozy shrugged. "We just went for a walk, that's all. It was a little crazy in the house, and we both wanted to get some fresh air."

"That was a lot of fresh air."

"We're talking about you, Grandma...not me," Cozy reminded.

"Well then...let's talk about something else," Dottie said, smiling. "How is work?"

Instantly, Cozy's stomach began to churn. "The same," she said. She wouldn't tell her grandmother about the new male customer who was harassing her at the café. Though Cozy confided nearly everything to her grandma, she wouldn't worry her with that. "Boring, stressful, and I hate it."

"I'm sorry, darling," Dottie said. "My offer still stands, you know—to help you with your school expenses so you can quit that awful job."

"I know, Grandma," Cozy said, smiling lovingly at her. "But I don't want to put you in a financial bind. I can handle it a little longer."

"Are you sure?"

"Of course. Most people hate their jobs. If I hang on long enough and get my degree, maybe I can get a job I won't hate so much. I'll certainly appreciate almost anything else after working at the café."

Dottie sighed. "Well…at least you're finished with making ornaments this year."

"That's true," Cozy said, smiling.

They were silent for a moment as Cozy fashioned a bow out of red ribbon and attached it to the newly wrapped gift in her lap. "There! That one came out very nicely, if I do say so myself."

"It's beautiful!" Dottie gushed. "How about we have some cider to celebrate its loveliness?"

"Great idea, Grandma," Cozy giggled. She thought about the conversation she'd had the day before with Jesse concerning her grandmother's cider and his grandfather's overactive bladder. It was romantic, in truth—Buck Bryant drinking gallons of cider just because he liked Dottie Robbins. It was hilarious as well.

"You know, Cozy," Dottie began, "Buck loves my cider! He just can't seem to get enough of it. I do wonder that the spices don't upset his stomach though."

Cozy smiled and followed her grandmother into the kitchen. She thought about sitting on the bench with Jesse beneath the canopy of gold created by the cottonwoods. What she wouldn't give to relive that moment.

She sighed and smiled. No matter what happened between her grandma and Buck Bryant, her

Thanksgiving Day walk with Jesse would forever be one of her most precious memories—of that she was absolutely certain.

The day after Thanksgiving came and went. Although Cozy had enjoyed her time with her grandmother—enjoyed listening to her favorite Christmas music, wrapping presents, and sipping cider—she felt a strange sort of emptiness wash over her. Black Friday had been the first day in a week that she hadn't seen Jesse, and she felt dissatisfied and lonesome.

Not only did the strange sense of absent joy linger all through the night, causing her sleep to be fitful and broken, it made the next day at work all the more difficult—especially when the creepy guy who had been giving her such a miserable time for over a week really stepped out of bounds in his treatment of her.

Still, as she drove to her grandmother's house after her shift, Cozy tried to put the latest incident out of her mind. She clung to the hope that Mr. Bryant and Jesse would drop in for the evening. Somehow she knew that just seeing Jesse, just being in the same room with him, would make her feel happier—more secure and not so alone.

Cozy nearly burst into tears of joy when she parked in front of her grandmother's house to see Jesse hunkered down before one of the animated deer in her grandma's yard. She was astonished at the emotions that broke over her—resplendent joy mingled with some sort of desperation. She suddenly wanted to jump out of her car, run to him, and tell him all about her horrible day at the café. She shook her head, trying to rattle some sense into her freaked-out brain. Was she losing it or something? She hardly knew the man! But there was something heroic about Jesse Bryant, something that inwardly whispered he would protect her if he could— or, in the very least, comfort her.

Still, Cozy knew she was out of control. So she inhaled a deep breath in an effort to calm her nerves, exhaling it slowly. She repeated the exercise five times in succession before stepping out of the car.

Jesse turned when he heard her car door close. "Hey, Little Red," he greeted with a smile.

"Hi," Cozy managed. She didn't know how she'd managed to respond to him—for she could have sworn her heart had leapt into her throat at the sound of his voice. She still wanted to run to him—even more than she had a moment before—but she forced herself to a normal pace of walking.

"Is something wrong with it?" she asked as she approached.

"Just a couple of bulbs that needed replacing," he said, standing up.

Cozy forced a conspiratorial smile. "Well? Are they inside...alone?" she asked.

"For the moment," he answered. "But I swear your grandma seemed nervous or something." He smiled then, adding, "And Grandpa has already been to the restroom twice."

Cozy covered her mouth as she burst into giggles.

"She's going to drown him!" she said, trying to settle her laughter.

"I know!" Jesse chuckled. The mirth evident in his fascinating blue eyes was like some healing potion, and Cozy immediately felt better—safe.

"Did you get it fixed, Jesse?"

Cozy and Jesse both tried to withhold more laughter as they looked to see Dottie standing on the front porch.

"I've got some fresh cider," she added.

Cozy heard Jesse choke on a chuckle, and she bit her lower lip hard to keep from giggling.

"Okay, Grandma," Cozy managed when she realized Jesse was too close to laughter to answer. "We're coming in."

"Good. I'll fill your mugs," Dottie chirped.

"I have to go to the bathroom already," Jesse mumbled.

Cozy couldn't keep from laughing, but managed to cover her mouth to muffle it.

As she and Jesse walked to the house, she said, "It's stuff like the cider that just makes me adore her all the more."

"She's hard to resist falling in love with, that's for sure," Jesse agreed.

Cozy smiled at him, thinking it was quite a wonderful thing he'd said about her grandmother. The thought also crossed her mind that she wished he felt the same way about her.

"Well, hey there, Cozy!" Mr. Bryant greeted from

the family room sofa as Jesse helped Cozy remove her coat.

"Hi, Mr. Bryant," she cheerfully greeted. Looking to Jesse, she said, "Thank you."

"My pleasure," Jesse said, winking at her. She thought her heart might burst right out of her chest. He was so gorgeous—such a gentleman! She'd never been treated so well by a man.

"Come on in, and have some cider with us, kids," Mr. Bryant said.

Cozy and Jesse exchanged amused grins. "Yes, let's," she giggled softly.

She shivered with euphoria as she felt Jesse place his hand on the small of her back to urge her into the family room. She was certain she was going to fly apart! Or in the very least that she was going to turn to him and confess her growing feelings for him. Still, she somehow managed to remain calm—or at least present the pretense of calm.

"Here you go, my darlings," Dottie said, offering a silver tray with four mugs on it to Cozy.

"Thanks, Grandma," Cozy said, taking a mug from the tray. She smiled as she watched her grandmother offer the tray to Buck and then Jesse.

Jesse winked at her, and she giggled.

"Ahh!" Dottie sighed as she sat down on the sofa next to Buck, her own mug in hand. "Sit down, kids," she said, smiling at them. "Buck built a fire, and I've got the candles on the mantel lit...lovely Christmas music in the background. It's perfect, isn't it?"

"Perfect," Buck said, winking at Cozy.

Cozy winked back at Buck, thinking he was cut from the same heroic cloth as his grandson. It would take a true hero to drink as much cider as her grandmother was constantly pouring down his throat—a very patient, understanding hero.

"So, Jesse," Dottie began then, "your grandpa says you put your Christmas tree up last night. How did Cozy's ornaments look on it?"

Cozy quickly looked to Jesse. Could it be that he really did put up a Christmas tree?

"Awesome," he said. "I should've bought more."

"Oh, good! And I'm sure Cozy has a few more she would—"

"Grandma!" Cozy scolded.

"Do you have any more?" he asked Cozy.

"Of course she does," Dottie answered for her granddaughter. "She always has extras. I do my whole tree with nothing but red glass ornaments and Cozy's walnuts. It's beautiful!"

"Why don't you tell Grandma about your raspberry almonds, Jesse?" Cozy interjected before the conversation could linger on her walnut ornaments any longer.

"Ooo! Raspberry almonds? Sounds simply tantalizing," Dottie breathed.

Touché, Buck mouthed to Cozy.

Jesse's eyes narrowed as he playfully glared at Cozy.

"Jesse says his raspberry almonds will change my life," Cozy added.

"Really?" Dottie asked with obvious delighted curiosity. "Do tell, Jesse."

Buck chuckled as Cozy offered Jesse a triumphant smile.

As Jesse began to explain to Dottie about the raspberry almonds he and his grandfather made each Christmas, Cozy sighed. She looked at the fire—the candle flames flickering inside the crackle-glass votives on the mantel. It was a warm and cozy scene, and she felt the stress of the day beginning to leave her body. She was glad to be there, right there with a grandmother who loved her and a potential grandfather who was charming and heroic—and the most wonderful man she had ever known.

Jesse grinned and tucked the five-dollar bill into the front pocket of his jeans. "Thanks, Grandpa," he said, restraining an amused chuckle.

"No. Thank *you*, son," Buck whispered with a wink.

Chuckling, Jesse left the hallway outside Dottie Robbins's bathroom and headed for her family room, where Cozy was relighting the candles on her grandmother's mantel. "Hey, Cozy," he said, still amused that his grandpa had bribed him in order to have some time alone with Dottie Robbins.

"Yeah?" Cozy asked, blowing out the match she'd been using.

"Do you wanna take a walk with me?" he asked, arching his brows and nodding toward the kitchen where his grandpa had rejoined Dottie.

A puzzled frown puckered Cozy's brows. Yet when Jesse again nodded toward the kitchen, Jesse saw understanding wash over her, and she smiled.

"Sure," she answered. "I could use a little walk."

"Cool," Jesse said, striding toward the door and retrieving Cozy's red coat from a hook. He chuckled again. He'd never imagined his grandpa could be such a player.

"Here you go, Little Red," Jesse said. A low growl rumbled in his throat as he helped Cozy on with her coat.

Cozy bit her lip with being overly delighted at his wolfishness. He winked at her as he took his barn jacket down from a hook and put it on.

"Are you ready?" he asked.

Cozy tried to keep her smile from stretching from ear to ear, but it was impossible. Another walk with Jesse Bryant? It was too surreal!

"Yep," she assured him as he opened the front door and gestured for her to precede him. "Thank you, Jesse."

"My pleasure, Cozy," he said.

"So," she began once he'd closed the door behind them, "you're already conniving to leave them alone with one another. You're a smart man."

But Jesse grinned, shaking his head. "Nope. My grandpa's a smart man," he said. "A little devious...but all's fair in love and war, they say."

"What do you mean?" They descended the front

porch steps, and Jesse fell into step beside her.

"He gave me five bucks to disappear so he can put the moves on your grandma," he told her.

Cozy's mouth dropped open in astonishment. "Seriously?" she giggled. "Are you kidding me?"

Jesse shook his head and chuckled. "Nope."

In truth, Cozy was severely disappointed to learn that Jesse had not truly wanted her to go for a walk with him—that he'd been bribed to do it. Still, she wouldn't let on.

"So...we've got five bucks. What do you want to do?" he asked.

"You actually accepted the five bucks?" Cozy asked as they passed through the gate and turned right. She was rendered breathless for a moment as he placed a hand on the small of her back to urge her forward.

"Of course," he answered. "I learned a long time ago that sometimes you need to let people give you things or do things for you...especially older people. He's never actually verbalized it, but I know Grandpa wants to feel like he's spoiling me. He didn't get to do that much spoiling when I was a kid. He was too busy helping Grandma to raise me. But he wants to be my grandpa now—you know, buy me things, give me five bucks to take a pretty girl out for...for whatever you can do for five bucks these days." He winked at her and smiled.

Cozy studied him a moment as they strolled down the leaf-littered sidewalk. It was such a sweet thing— his grandpa giving him money to get out of the house.

She had no reason to allow her feelings to be hurt. Furthermore, she suddenly realized how wise Jesse had been to accept the five bucks.

"So you're telling me that every time my grandma buys me something I don't need…that I should just be way excited about it instead of scolding her for doing it?" she ventured.

"Yeah," Jesse confirmed. "I know with Grandpa, it takes the joy out of giving me whatever it is he's giving me if I make a fuss or tell him he doesn't need to spend his money on me. I've learned just to let him give." He smiled again—a somewhat melancholy smile. "After all, who knows how many more years I have with him? So I don't see any reason to make him feel bad about spoiling me a little."

Cozy sighed, looked down, and watched her own feet crunching brittle leaves as she walked. "You *are* a smart guy," she said—and it was true.

"Not really," Jesse mumbled. "I can just read Grandpa's expressions…like a book. He's not as good at guarding them as he used to be."

Cozy was awed with Jesse insight, thoughtfulness, and humility. He was absolutely right. She thought about how excited her Grandma always got whenever she was presenting Cozy with some little something she'd picked up with Cozy in mind—or some big something. She thought about the thirty or more different crackle-glass votives and candle holders she owned, all lovingly given to her by her grandma. A vision of the pure joy evident on Dottie Robbins's face

135

whenever she watched Cozy open a new box of crackle glass lingered in her mind, and in that very moment, she vowed never to put up a fuss again. The next time her grandma spent too much money on her or gave her something—anything at all—she'd do nothing but express her delight and appreciation. For a moment, she let her thoughts linger on the fact that her beloved grandmother would be gone one day—and that when she was, Cozy could sit in her home (wherever it happened to be), watch the tiny flames flicker in the pretty crackle-glass votives—watch the lacy shadows they cast dance on the wall—and remember how much her grandma loved her.

She quickly changed her train of thought, however, for tears were welling in her eyes, and she didn't want to appear too sappy in front of Jesse. The lousy day she'd had at work did nothing to strengthen her, however, and she truly had to struggle to keep her composure.

Still, she obviously hadn't struggled hard enough, for in the next moment, Jesse asked, "Are you okay?"

"Oh, yeah," Cozy fibbed, shrugging her shoulders. "Just thinking about what you said…and I sort of had a lousy day at work. I guess I'm just a little tired."

"A lousy day at work?" he pressed. "Why?"

A breath of nervous laughter escaped her lungs, and she shook her head. "Nothing out of the ordinary. Just the regular junk. I can't wait until I'm finished with school. Then I hope I never have to waitress again."

"What happened?" he asked.

She looked up to him to find he was frowning.

He wore an expression of genuine concern, and Cozy's heart did a little flip-flop inside her chest. He was so handsome! Jesse Bryant was so very classically handsome that Cozy could hardly believe he was giving her the time of day.

"We're out for a refreshing walk, with five whole bucks burning a hole in your pocket," she said, smiling at him. "Why on earth would I want to tell you about my lousy day at work...with all this to wipe my worries away?" She inhaled a deep breath of crisp, late autumn evening air and sighed.

Jesse's frown relaxed and then disappeared. His perfect lips curved and parted to reveal his movie-star smile.

"Okay," he said. He nodded in the direction before them. "There's that little coffee shop and bakery up here about a mile. Are you up for hot chocolate or something?"

Cozy giggled. "Ooo!" she cooed. "Maybe we could share a hot chocolate and have enough money left over to split one of those big iced sugar cookies they sell!"

Jesse laughed. "Yeah. I like those big cookies they have there."

"Me too," Cozy admitted. "I've been going there with Grandma as long as I can remember. I think one of my first memories is of her and Mom pushing me in the stroller when I was little and going to Bea's Bakery for a cookie."

"Bea's Bakery?" he asked.

Cozy shrugged. "Yeah," she sighed. "It used to

be called Bea's Bakery back then. It was just a bakery, without a coffee shop and tables like it has now."

"I didn't know that."

"But," Cozy continued, raising an index finger for dramatics, "when Miss Bea sold the bakery about five years ago, the guy who bought it kept her son on as the baker in the coffee shop. So that's why the good cookies are still so good there."

"Wow! You really know stuff," Jesse said, a lilt of admiration in his voice.

"Oh, I know a lot of stuff," Cozy confirmed. "None of it is of any value, of course...but I do know stuff."

"Such as?" Jesse prodded with an amused chuckle.

"Such as...did you know that crayons are one of the top ten most recognizable scents to American adults...and that smelling them has been proven to lower stress?" she offered.

Jesse laughed again. "I'm not too proud to admit that I did not know that."

"Well, now you do...which means you know stuff too."

"Awesome," he chuckled. "I've always wanted to know stuff."

"Then I'm your source," Cozy giggled, smiling at him. "If you ever want to know stuff...just ask me."

"Okay then. Tell me some more stuff."

Cozy shook her head at her own stupid babble. Still, he did seem sincerely interested. "Okay...um... let's see. Did you know that the dial tone of a normal telephone is in the key of F? Or that the first item ever scanned and sold with a UPC barcode was a package of Wrigley's Juicy Fruit gum?"

"Really?" he asked.

"Yep. At a grocery store in Troy, Ohio, on June 26, 1974," Cozy confirmed. "It is now on display at the Smithsonian."

"Yeah, I'd say you know stuff all right," Jesse chuckled.

"Yes. I'm a living abyss of pointless crapola."

Jesse laughed. She was hilarious—hilarious and completely adorable! She was far too attractive for her own good too. He studied her for a moment—watched her sliding her feet through the dry, brittle leaves as they walked.

"I can never remember stuff like that," he admitted.

"Maybe not," she said, smiling at him. "But you're wicked good at putting up Christmas lights."

"Oh, yeah. That's important," he chuckled with sarcasm. "Something I need to be sure to include on my résumé...or if I ever sign up for one of those online dating things."

She giggled, and his ears liked the sound of it. "Actually, if you want to know a secret...it's exactly something you should put on your profile if you ever do sign up for one."

"You're kidding."

She shook her head. "Nope. Women love it when men do dangerous things like climbing around on the roof to put up Christmas lights. They find it very attractive."

Jesse laughed heartily then. "Okay, look...I already promised to buy you hot chocolate and a cookie. You don't have to butter me up or try to inflate my ego. The five bucks is as good as spent."

She laughed but assured him, "But I'm serious! It's...it's heroic."

"You really want that cookie bad, don't you?" he teased. Still, he could tell she really meant what she'd said.

"Well, yes...but that's not why I said it."

He shook his head, amused by her dramatics. Did she really think that a man putting up some stupid Christmas lights was heroic?

"So tell me, why is putting up Christmas lights considered heroic to girls?" he couldn't resist asking. "And don't try to tell me it's because it's dangerous."

"Well, first of all," she began, "it is dangerous. Do you know how many people are hurt every year while trying to put Christmas lights on a house?"

"No...and if you tell me you do know, I'll—"

"Hospital emergency rooms treat approximately twelve thousand five hundred injuries every year related to holiday decorating," she interrupted.

"You're kidding," he said. In truth, he was astonished—not that she knew the number, but that the number was so high.

"Nope," she assured him. "However, even though risking life and limb to put up Christmas lights is totally manly, what makes it heroic is that most men do it even when they don't want to. You know…for their wives and children…their mothers." She paused, looked at him, and smiled. "Their grandpas and grandmas…and neighbors."

Jesse could tell Cozy was entirely sincere. Yet he couldn't let her know just how good she'd made him feel by implying he was heroic in her estimation. She'd think he was a shallow idiot for sure.

"Well…I guess I better add it to my online dating profile then," he said.

"Are you serious?" she asked, and he laughed when he saw the look of concern on her face. "You have an online dating profile?"

"What do you think?" he asked, winking at her.

Cozy would never tell him what she really thought of him—that she knew a man like him would have no need of any kind of dating service, online or otherwise. Instead she decided to admit her remorse at revealing the whole Christmas light scenario.

"I think I shouldn't have told you that women find it attractive when men string Christmas lights all over the outside of a house," she mumbled.

"Why not?" he asked, still smiling.

"Because now that you know it, you'll probably go out and use it to your advantage," she said. "I'll probably start seeing beautiful Christmas light displays all over down here in the valley by the river…and all the houses that are lit up will be owned by gorgeous, movie-star-type single women who met you on some dating website." He laughed, and she added, "However, I should warn you that once a woman knows your heroics are contrived, they cease to think they're attractive."

"You mean, if I started wooing women with my awesome Christmas lights displays, they'd eventually wise up that I was doing it on purpose and dump me?" he asked.

"Exactly."

Cozy loved the sound of Jesse's chuckle—the way it rumbled deep in his broad chest and then rose to his throat.

"When we get back, I'm going to tell Grandpa that this was the best five bucks he ever spent on my education," Jesse said, smiling at her.

"I'm sure that it is," she giggled. "And you'll never look at crayons the same way again either."

"That's true," he said. "I should buy a box and keep them in my office at work...just for those extra stressful days."

"Yes, you should," she confirmed.

Suddenly, Jesse inhaled a deep breath, exhaling it with a contented sigh. "Mm! I can smell the bakery already. Do you smell it?"

Cozy inhaled—caught the light aroma of baking bread on the evening air. "Yeah! It's making me salivate already."

Jesse bit his tongue as the thought traveled through

his mind, *And you're making me salivate already, Cozy Robbins.*

CHAPTER SEVEN

"So?" Dottie asked. "What do you think they're doing right about now?"

Buck smiled. "Well, if I taught that boy right, he oughta have that girl backed up against a tree somewhere, kissing her like there's no tomorrow." He laughed when Dottie's pretty blue eyes lit up like the Fourth of July sky over the Hudson River.

"Really?" she asked, awash with delight.

Buck chuckled. "No. Jesse's enough of a gentleman to move a little more carefully than that," he said. "At least...I think he is."

Dottie sighed with disappointment. "It's too bad, really. Cozy needs a good, wet, driven kiss from that boy."

"Oh, does she now?" Buck asked. He liked this woman—liked her much more than she could possibly imagine. "From Jesse and only Jesse?"

"Yep," Dottie assured him. "Cozy has been waiting her whole life for your Jesse, Buck. I know it sounds ridiculous—and I don't want you to think I'm crazy or anything—but...but I can see it in her. I can see it in him."

Buck smiled, reached across the table, and covered Dottie's hand with his own. "So can I, Dottie."

"Really?" she asked.

He could read the relief in her expression—and the hope.

Buck nodded and said, "The night you and Cozy came over with the banana bread...well...you'll never know how glad I was to see you...and how glad I was to see that girl of yours. Jesse's attention was on her the whole time you were at the house that night, and I thought, *Finally*! *Finally that boy's going to give his heart away.* He's been holding onto it real tight for a very long time."

"I'm glad he has," Dottie confessed. "And I hope you're right. I hope we both are."

"We are, Dottie. Just give it time."

Her face softened, and her eyes twinkled as she gazed at him across the table. "You're saying we just have to be patient...and...and let things take their natural course."

"Yep," Buck said—and he knew they were no longer talking about Jesse and Cozy.

"Well, then," she sighed, picking up her mug of cider with her free hand, "I'll try not to worry too much."

"Don't worry at all, Dottie," Buck said with a wink. "Everything will turn out just as it's meant to."

"Why won't you tell me?" Jesse asked as he leaned back in his chair and studied Cozy for a moment.

She shrugged—frowned. "Because it's not important. You have bad days at work, don't you?"

"Well, sure. But this seems different. This seems like…I don't know…like it's kind of eating you up or something."

Cozy shook her head. She couldn't tell him. He'd think she was a total dork. Anyway, it wouldn't change anything. The creep would still come in every day at noon—still do what he'd been doing for over a week.

"Come on," he prodded. "Just tell me. Maybe I can help."

Cozy bit her lip. He couldn't help. Still, she sensed it was important to him—that he wanted her to confide in him. And in truth, something in her did want to tell someone—to tell him.

"It's just that…it's sort of ongoing, and I don't really see how it's going to change…and I'm…I'm uncomfortable with it," she confessed at last.

Jesse frowned and leaned forward in his chair. Cozy broke another piece off the large sugar cookie on the plate in the middle of the table. She and Jesse had finished the hot chocolate long before but were still picking at the cookie.

"Can I get you anything else, sir?" Cozy glanced up to the waitress. She looked to be about sixteen and was nearly panting over Jesse.

"Um…yeah," he answered. "Can we get two ice waters and a warm cider?"

"Sure," the girl said, smiling. "I'll have them right out to you."

"Thanks," Jesse said, returning his attention to Cozy. "Now tell me. What's this ongoing thing at work that's putting that frown on your pretty little forehead?"

Cozy smiled. "Now who's buttering who up?" she teased him.

But he didn't smile. "I'm serious. Tell me."

She couldn't look him in the eye for some reason. So she simply picked at the cookie again.

"Well, there's this guy," she began. "He started coming in about two weeks ago...every day for lunch."

"And?" he urged.

"He's gross, you know," she continued. "Like maybe midthirties. He's all beefed up and thinks he's God's gift to women. Anyway, he started sitting at one of my tables about ten days ago. And he's...you know... disgusting. Like he says stuff...gross stuff to me. And he always finds a way to, like, pinch my bum or brush his arm against my...my chest."

"Well, give him a knee in the guy-junk!" Jesse exclaimed, suddenly angry. "You don't take that from any man...from anybody at all, Cozy!"

She was surprised by his sudden protective outburst—flattered too, however.

"I know," she said, shaking her head. "But jobs are so hard to find right now...and if I can stick this one out for another two semesters, then hopefully I won't have to—"

"I'm gonna come over there to that café and kick his ass," Jesse growled.

Cozy looked up to him, astonished at the indignant rage on his face. "No! No, no! It's fine. I can take care of it," she assured him. "I know I should tell Blake. He's my manager...but..."

"But what?" he pressed.

"Well, the last time my friend Mindy complained about a customer, Blake told her she should be flattered and reminded her that the guy left her a big tip and to be grateful for it. So I've just been kind of hoping it would go away somehow."

"Well, I was hoping the big zit on my right cheek would go away before high school senior prom too, Cozy," he growled. "But it didn't...not until I rubbed it off with some sandpaper and made it bleed. You can't let somebody treat you like that. Women put up with enough sh—stuff. You need to put an end to it."

"You did what?" she asked. "Did you say you sandpapered a zit?"

Jesse shrugged, though it was obvious he was still angry. "Yeah...I sanded it off. So what?"

"You sanded it off? Didn't it bleed?"

"Well, yeah...but I figured that a scraped-up, scabby sore looked better than a zit." He paused a moment, shaking his head and trying to calm his temper. "Seriously, Cozy. I know women like to be strong and independent and all...but you can't let this guy do that again. Promise me you won't tolerate it anymore. Hell...I'll give you a job at my company if that's what you're worried about."

Cozy almost smiled. She knew she should probably be disturbed that Jesse had become so instantly angry, but she wasn't. She was flattered—pleased even. She felt validated and empowered somehow. He was right. She should never allow herself to be treated with such disrespect—never let anyone get away with touching her in any manner she deemed inappropriate.

"You're right," she said. "You're right. I guess I just...I don't know. I guess I just—"

"You're worried about your job," he finished. "And I get that. Jobs *are* hard to come by just now. But you've got plenty of family and friends that would help you out. And anyway, if your boss fires you for that...then I'll kick his ass too."

"Shhh!" Cozy hushed him, reaching out to place her hand over his mouth. "It's all right. I'll take care of it. I will. You're right. I shouldn't have put up with it at all...not one minute. I've just been so busy and stressed with my ornaments and stuff."

Jesse exhaled a heavy sigh. "I'm sorry," he said. "I just get ticked off with things like this." He shook his head again—rubbed his chin with one hand as if trying to settle himself further. "It's just that...well, I wanna grab your butt every time I see you too...but that doesn't mean I act on it."

Cozy looked up when the waitress cleared her throat to arrest Jesse's attention.

"Here you go, sir," the girl said, setting the two

waters and a mug of cider on the table.

"Thanks," Jesse mumbled without looking at her.

The waitress's eyebrows arched, and she looked to Cozy. Obviously she had heard what Jesse had said about wanting to pinch her butt every time he saw her—and Cozy was glad she had.

"Let me know if you need anything else," the waitress said.

"We will. Thanks," Cozy assured her with a smile.

"Promise me, Cozy," Jesse said, having finally lowered his voice. "Promise me you won't put up with it again...even if you get fired."

"I promise," she whispered.

"I don't believe you," he said. His eyes narrowed as he studied her for a moment.

"I promise," she reiterated. "Now come on. Help me drink this cider. And don't make me wish I hadn't told you."

He nodded and rubbed his whiskers again. Sighing, he mumbled, "And I'm sorry, but I cuss when I get mad."

"It's okay," she said. In truth, she was outrageously pleased that he had come to her defense so instantly and with such vehemence. "And you are right. I don't know what's been the matter with me."

She watched as he broke off a piece of the cookie and shoved it in his mouth. "It's just what you said... stress."

Cozy stared at him for a long moment. It was

obvious he was still riled up, but he was settling down quickly.

"Did you really sandpaper off a zit just because of prom?" she asked.

"Oh, yeah," he answered. He didn't crack a smile—as if using sandpaper to remove a pimple were the most natural thing in the world. "I just told everybody I wiped out on my dirt bike."

"Guys are so funny," Cozy sighed, shaking her head. She giggled a little, thinking of an adolescent Jesse Bryant taking a piece of sandpaper to his face.

"No...guys are just stupid," he said. "For instance," he added, grinning at her, "now everyone in here knows I've checked out your butt...and more than once."

"That was just the sugar talking," she said, pointing to the cookie remains on the plate.

He chuckled. "Nope. I'm afraid that was just me revealing too much while under the influence of testosterone."

"Well, I'll tell you what," Cozy began, picking up the mug of cider and taking a long sip.

"What's that?" he asked, breaking off another piece of the cookie.

"On the way home, I'll check out your butt, and then we'll be even." She smiled at him, and her heart leapt when he smiled back.

"You'd have to ogle it all the way home to catch up, Cozy Robbins," he countered.

Cozy laughed and took another sip of the cider.

She offered the mug to him, and he nodded,

accepting it and taking a sip. "It's good," he said. "But not as good as your grandmother's."

"What do you think our grandparents are doing right now?" Cozy asked. Jesse returned the mug to her, and she took another sip of the warm, soothing cider.

Jesse smiled. "I don't know," he answered. "But whatever they're doing, I hope it was worth five bucks."

Cozy laughed in her throat, covering her mouth to keep from spitting cider across the table.

Jesse smiled his dazzling smile and broke off another piece of the sugar cookie. "Are you really going to check out my butt on the way home?" he teased.

Again Cozy nearly spit the cider out of her mouth. Once she'd managed to swallow, she giggled, "Sure. If it'll make you feel better."

"I don't know. Now I'm kind of self-conscious."

"I hope you know the Heimlich…because you're gonna make me choke if you keep it up," Cozy warned, dapping at a dribble of cider that had escaped onto her chin when she'd laughed.

Jesse glanced around the café. "It looks like they're getting ready to close up. We should probably go."

"Yeah," Cozy said, pushing her chair away from the table.

"Do you want the rest of that?" Jesse asked, pointing to the remains of the cookie.

"No, that's okay. It was good though, huh?"

"Oh, yeah," he said. She smiled as he picked up the biggest piece left and stuffed it in his mouth. "After you." He nodded toward the door, and Cozy started walking.

"Have a nice night," the waitress called.

Looking over her shoulder, Cozy said, "You too. Thanks."

As she stepped outside, the cold night air hit her like an unexpected assault, and she shivered. "Brrr! I should've taken my coat off while we were in there," she said, rubbing her arms.

"Do you wanna wait here and I'll run home and get my truck?" Jesse asked.

"Oh, no. I'll be fine once we start walking," she assured him.

"Are you sure?"

"Yeah."

As they started back up the sidewalk, Cozy smiled when Jesse stepped around behind her to place himself between her and the road. She wondered if he did it consciously or if it was just habit for him. Either way, it was chivalrous.

"Brr!" he shuddered. "It is getting cold."

"I guess winter's on its way." Cozy drew a deep breath. She could smell the frost in the air and savored the sound of the leaves crunching beneath their feet as they walked.

They talked as they walked—about nothing and yet everything—and Cozy inwardly admitted that she simply loved the sound of Jesse's voice. It had the same effect on her other four senses as her grandmother's mulled cider had on her sense of taste. It soothed and comforted her—made her feel warm, safe, and content. His wit caused her to laugh more than once, and she realized then that before meeting Jesse Bryant she had often bottled up her laughter—that she'd somehow grown uncomfortable about letting herself laugh unrestrained. She studied him for a moment. Jesse Bryant made her a better person. He encouraged and empowered her—treated her as she felt a woman should be treated. It was another hero quality he possessed.

All too soon, the bright and beautiful lighting displays of the Bryant's and Robbins's houses came into view. A melancholy disappointment began to seep into Cozy's veins as she realized her time alone with Jesse was almost at an end. She frowned, thinking it was strange, for she'd never before in her entire life experienced even a moment of disappointment at arriving at her grandmother's house. It disturbed her.

"Do you think it's safe for us to approach?" Jesse asked, slowing their pace to a snail's crawl.

Cozy smiled. "Why wouldn't it be?" she asked.

Jesse shrugged. "I don't know. They might be, like… you know…cuddling on the couch or something."

Cozy giggled. "So?"

He took hold of her arm and stopped her advancement toward her grandmother's. "Thanks for being willing to waste your night with me," he said.

"What are you talking about?" she asked, smiling. "I had fun. You were the one who had to be bribed into going. I went because I wanted to."

"It would take a lot more than five bucks to bribe me into doing anything," he said. "You know that, right?"

"I suppose so," she said, even though doubt still pecked at her insecurities.

"No...really," he said. "You do know I wanted to go for a walk with you anyway, right?"

She nodded. "I do," she fibbed.

A fascinating grin of mischief slowly spread across his handsome face. "You do know how cute you look in your Little Red Riding Hood outfit, don't you? With Jack Frost nipping at your nose and everything?"

"Is my nose red?" she asked, worried that she might look more like Rudolph rather than Little Red Riding Hood.

"No," he mumbled.

Cozy's eyes widened as Jesse's head descended toward hers. She held her breath as he placed a soft, warm kiss to the tip of her nose.

"But it's cold," he said.

Goose bumps raced over Cozy's arms as a tidal wave of intense bliss consumed her. She shivered from the sensation of it.

Misunderstanding the reaction of her body to his flirting, Jesse asked, "Are you that cold?"

"Just a little chilly," she fibbed again.

Jesse's eyes narrowed—smoldered with some sort of provocative invitation Cozy couldn't translate.

"Well then, let me warm you up a bit," he said, taking her face between his hands.

Cozy gasped as she felt the warmth of his lips against her own. She was certain she would faint when he kissed her again—but she didn't—and her eyes closed as Jesse kissed her a third time, his lips lingering warm and moist against hers. Over and over he kissed her—each kiss lingering longer than the one before.

After a few long moments of raining bliss over her, he paused, tracing her lips with his thumbs. "Is that too wolfish of me, Little Red?" he asked in a low, provocative tone that caused her to shiver.

"No," she breathed.

"Good," he said. "Because it seems to me that you're still a little too chilly."

"Probably," she whispered, nodding.

"Let me take care of that for you."

Mustering every ounce of gentlemanly self-control he could, Jesse kissed Cozy Robbins again—kissed her softly—restrained the passion shouting at him to kiss her harder—more intimately. This was their first kiss, and he wanted it to be memorable for her—wanted her to enjoy it more than she'd ever enjoyed kissing any other man. So he concentrated on her—on Cozy and what he felt she needed after dealing with a freaking pervert at work. She needed tenderness, reassurance—slow, easy affection that wasn't forced and selfish.

Therefore, though it took every bit of strength he had, Jesse kissed her tenderly. Oh, there was still enough physical desire evident in the way he kissed her to assure her that he'd like nothing more than to attack

157

her—but he mingled it with enough self-control to prove to her he could protect her, even from himself.

It was then that he was sure. He'd never in his life felt so protective of a woman—never wanted to spend every waking moment with just one person—spend every sleeping moment with her. It was in that moment—as Cozy Robbins's arms slipped around his waist, as she melted against him, trusting him—it was in that moment that he knew for certain. He was in love with her.

Jesse's body was warm and seemed to invite Cozy's to share that warmth. She wanted to keep him—to marry him—to own his heart and attention forever! Cozy knew she was crazy, but she couldn't help the way she felt. She was in love with him, and she couldn't change it, even if she'd wanted to—which she didn't. She wondered for a moment how she could be in love with a man she'd only known for a matter of days—literally, days! Yet as he pulled her into his arms, still kissing her as she'd never been kissed before, she didn't care what anybody else would think were she to confess that she loved him. She loved him—whether it was crazy or not.

All too soon, his kisses lightened. He was going to stop kissing her, and Cozy wanted to scream—beg him not to stop—but she knew he really would think she'd lost her mind then. So, as his embrace slacked, she released him—blushing for the fact that she knew her delight was all too evident on her countenance.

"You don't want to tempt me too much, Little

Red," he said, smiling at her. "A wolf is wolf no matter how he tries to convince you otherwise."

She smiled at him. "Oh, you can huff and puff all you want, Mr. Wolf," she began, "but you're not fooling me. You're just a big puppy dog at heart."

He grinned, shrugging his broad shoulders. "Maybe I am," he chuckled. "Or maybe I'm just trying to lull you into a false sense of security so that you'll venture farther away from the fire and be easy prey."

Cozy giggled—linked her arm with his. "Well, I'll take my chances," she said as they started toward home. "After all, you still haven't eaten up my granny and put on her nightgown."

He laughed. "If I ever put on your granny's nightgown, you shoot me there on the spot, baby!"

Jesse pulled his arm away from hers, placing it about her shoulders and pulling her closer against him. "Now, let's get home and check on those two teenagers back at the house before they get into any trouble."

"Or before your grandpa's bladder bursts," Cozy offered.

"Exactly!" Jesse laughed.

He started to whistle—"Li'l Red Riding Hood," of course—and Cozy giggled when he paused long enough to allow a low growl to rumble in his chest.

"Here they come!" Dottie whispered from her place kneeling on the floor in front of the picture window.

"Where?" Buck asked, adjusting his binoculars.

"To the right…just before your house. See them?"

"Now I do." Buck chuckled. "They look awful cozy, don't they?"

"Indeed they do," Dottie sighed. Putting down her binoculars, she struggled to her feet, wincing with embarrassment as her knees cracked. "Now hurry! Let's get on into the kitchen so they don't suspect anything."

"I'm trying, woman!" Buck laughed as he struggled to his feet.

Dottie giggled when she heard Buck's knees crack louder than hers had.

"Oh, no!" Dottie squealed in a whisper. "We left the binoculars in the front room!"

"I tossed a newspaper over them," Buck said. "We're fine."

Dottie laughed as she handed Buck a mug full of now-cold cider. "Aren't we a pair?" she giggled. "Like two spies on a mission."

"Well, honey...that's exactly what we are," Buck said, winking at her. "And it looks like our mission is about to be a success."

Dottie sighed with hopeful contentment as she and Buck clicked their mugs together to toast their triumph so far. Oh, how she loved to look at the handsome man who lived next door. She wished she could look at him for the rest of her life—sit at the kitchen table and know he would always be sitting across from her. But this was Cozy's time for love, and Dottie was bound and determined to make sure her sweet girl didn't miss out on it.

"We're home," Cozy called as the front door opened.

"We're in here," Dottie called. "Did you have a nice walk?"

"We sure did," Cozy answered as she stepped into the kitchen with Jesse at her heels. Her cheeks were as red as summer cherries—and Dottie knew it wasn't from the cold. The boy had finally kissed her!

"Wonderful!" Dottie sighed. "That's just wonderful!"

CHAPTER EIGHT

"Are you Mindy?" Jesse asked the girl at the register. She wasn't wearing a nametag, but she was the only other young waitress in the place. Deductive reasoning told Jesse this was Mindy, Cozy's friend from work. "Is Cozy working right now?"

The girl looked up, her eyes widening to the size of flying saucers. Her mouth hung open for a moment as if she'd just seen an extraterrestrial.

"Y-you must be Jesse," the girl managed to stammer.

Jesse grinned, more than merely pleased that Cozy had obviously told her friend about his existence. He glanced at the clock on the wall. It was high noon.

"Is Cozy working right now?" he repeated. "And is that idiot guy here?"

The girl nodded. "Yes and yes," she answered.

"Where is he?"

"He's sitting over there…in that corner," Mindy said, pointing to a table across the room.

Jesse's gaze looked to the table she indicated. He exhaled a heavy breath as he looked at the creep sitting at the corner table.

"Fair warning," Mindy whispered then. "Our manager will call the cops if you cause a scene."

Jesse shrugged. "I'm not gonna cause a scene. I'm just gonna lay him out if he touches her again," he said.

Mindy smiled and bit her lip with delighted anticipation. "Then I'll stick around a minute."

"You do that," Jesse said, winking at her. He leaned on the counter, studying the man. "Let me ask you this, Mindy," he began.

"Yeah?"

"Will you be okay here if Cozy gets fired today?"

Mindy nodded. "Absolutely."

"Good."

Jesse knew Cozy well enough to know she would worry about her friend. He thought it best to know just how loyal a friend Mindy was—just in case the jerk really did have the nerve to molest Cozy right in front of him.

"Here she comes," Mindy whispered.

Jesse looked across the room to see Cozy making her way toward the guy's table with a plate of food in her hand. He clenched his teeth and inhaled a deep breath to calm himself. He'd wait—wait and see if she could handle it on her own. But if she couldn't...

"There she goes," Mindy said quietly.

Jesse watched Cozy put the plate on the table in front of the degenerate. His muscles tensed, and he took a step forward when the man reached out and brushed a hand over Cozy's rear end. Barely able to restrain himself, he held his breath as he watched her back away from the man and slap his hand away when he tried to take hold of her arm.

"Good, good," he breathed, struggling to keep from leaping over tables and chairs to get to her. "You tell him, girl. You tell him no."

The man reached for her again, however, and as she pushed at his hand again, the creep reached down, running his hand over the outside of her thigh.

"Oh no, you don't, man," Jesse growled.

"Sir?" some guy called as Jesse stormed toward the table where the jerk had taken hold of Cozy's wrist. "Sir? This is none of your business." Jesse shoved the little wimp calling him *sir* into a table when the weenie tried to step in front of him.

"Get your hands off her!" Jesse growled as he finally reached Cozy. Taking hold of her arm, he pulled her aside and away from the creep sitting at the table.

"Jesse," Cozy breathed.

"You don't treat a woman like that," he said through clenched teeth, however.

"And who are you, pretty boy?" the man said, pushing his chair away from the table and standing up.

Cozy was awash with mingled fear and pride. Jesse had come for her! He was championing her. It was wonderful—wonderful and awful! Wonderful because it was proof he cared for her—awful because she knew it could mean trouble for him.

She heard Jesse call the man a strong synonym for *jerk* and gasped when the man swore back at him.

"Now gentlemen," Blake said as he approached, "let's not have any trouble here."

Jesse looked to Blake, scowling with disgust. "I should kick your butt too," he said. "You should be protecting your employees from this kind of sh— stuff...so that I don't have to."

Cozy screamed as the creep she'd been serving lunch to threw a sucker punch at Jesse while he was looking at Blake. Jesse was quick, but the man's fist still grazed his right cheek.

"You don't wanna start something with me, dude. I promise you that," Jesse threatened. "You may start it...but you sure as hell can believe I'll finish it."

"Well, come on then, movie star," the letch taunted. "Let's see what you have."

"Jesse?" Cozy breathed.

The creep threw another punch, and she gasped, covering her mouth with her hands. Jesse easily caught the man's fist with one hand, however, landing his own punch to the man's jaw with his other. The man stumbled back, looking stunned for a moment before he aggressed again.

"Don't do it, man," Jesse warned, shaking his head.

But the creep lunged at Jesse anyway. Jesse easily evaded the man's fist again and then took hold of the guy's shoulders, pulling him down so that his midsection met with Jesse's knee. The man doubled over for only a moment before straightening up again.

Cozy watched, tears spilling from her eyes as the jerk raised his fists like a boxer as Jesse shook his head.

"Really?" Jesse asked.

"Bring it on," the man growled.

Jesse inhaled a deep breath and struck. Cozy startled as his fist hit the man's jaw with brutal force, sending him sprawling to the floor.

"You need to leave," Blake shouted at Jesse. "Now!"

"You got it, you piece of—"

"Jesse!" Cozy exclaimed, taking hold of his arm.

Jesse looked to her, inhaled a deep breath, and nodded to her.

"Come on," he said, taking hold of her arm.

"And where do you think you're going, Cozy?" Blake asked her.

"She quits, man. And you can kiss my—" Jesse began.

"Let's go, Jesse," Cozy said. Jesse let go of her arm, and she quickly removed her apron, angrily tossing it at Blake. "Jerk," she spat at him.

She felt Jesse's hand at the small of her back and turned to leave. She blushed as everyone else in the café started applauding as they left.

Call me later, for sure! Mindy mouthed, making the universal signal of thumb to ear and pinky to mouth to indicate a phone.

I will, Cozy mouthed, nodding to her friend.

As Jesse escorted Cozy to her car, she heard him exhale a heavy sigh. He took hold of her arm and pulled her to a stop. She turned to face him and could see the mixed emotions playing out on his expression.

"Are you mad at me for this?" he asked.

It seemed a billion thoughts were crashing around in her head all at once. She knew the politically correct answer, but she was sick of political correctness—sick of the way that society emasculated men and defeminized women. Furthermore, she saw nothing standing before her but pure masculine, old-fashioned, vanishing heroism.

"The truth?" she asked.

He sighed, nodding as if he dreaded her answer.

"Society would say I should be angry," she began, "but I'm not."

"You're not?" he asked as if he couldn't believe her answer.

She shook her head. "No."

"But I just lost my cool...*and* I quit your job for you," he reminded her.

She smiled, reached up, and put a palm to his square five-o'clock-shadowed jaw. "My hero," she sighed dramatically.

"Really?" he asked.

"Yeah," she assured him. Her smile broadened then as she said, "Though...if I was a good girl, I'd work on that potty mouth of yours."

Jesse grinned, and butterflies swarmed in Cozy's stomach as mischief instantly leapt to his gorgeous eyes. "You can work on my mouth anytime, baby," he said.

"Ooo!" she cooed. "Very wolfish, Mr. Bryant."

"You like that, do you?" he chuckled.

"I like *you*," she whispered, raising herself on her tiptoes and placing a kiss on his cheek. She knew better than to admit how very, very much she liked his playing at being akin to a wolf, however—lest he start contriving ways to play at it instead of just letting it happen naturally.

"Well, I like you too, Little Red," he said, winking at her. He took her chin in his hand and placed a very warm and moist kiss to her lips. "But I gotta get back to work now or those three little pigs downtown won't have their Christmas lights up in time."

"Okay," Cozy sighed.

"Are you going over to your grandma's house tonight?" he asked.

"Of course," she answered—though Cozy had begun to wonder if she was spending every evening at her grandmother's house with the intention of making sure everything kept progressing between her grandma and Mr. Bryant or whether she simply couldn't keep away from Jesse any longer.

"Then I'll see you later," he said.

"Definitely," Cozy sighed.

"First unlock your car door so I can be sure you get out of here safely," he instructed.

"Okay."

Cozy reached into her pocket and pushed the button on her car key. She was glad she always kept her purse in the trunk of her car instead of in the café lockers. It had made leaving very smooth.

Jesse opened the driver's side door, and Cozy slid into her seat. "Drive safe," he said.

"You too," she told him.

He closed the door, and she smiled when she heard him start to whistle the familiar Sam the Sham and the Pharaohs tune.

Jesse watched Cozy drive out of the café parking lot before heading to his truck. He knew that, in the eyes of the world, he'd acted like a Neanderthal by confronting the guy in the café—but he didn't care. All he knew was that Cozy was out of a miserable situation and that she was glad he'd done what he'd done. That was all that mattered to him.

"Cozy Robbins," he breathed as he got into his truck and started the engine. "Girl, you've got me twisted around your little finger, and you don't even know it, do you?" he chuckled. "I may be a wolf," he said to himself, "but you're taming me fast, Little Red Riding Hood. You're taming me fast."

"Ooo, I love it!" Dottie exclaimed. "Jesse defending your honor? How romantic!"

Cozy smiled. "I know, huh?" Cozy sighed as she twisted her mug where it sat on her grandmother's table. "I-I probably should've at least *acted* a little more remorseful," she said.

"Why?" Dottie asked. "Did you feel remorseful over what Jesse did?"

"Not at all," Cozy confessed.

"Then you shouldn't have acted like you did. That wouldn't have been being true to yourself. And besides...men need to slay dragons," Dottie said. "Half the problem in this country is that men are expected to be happy with just stepping on ants when their very nature is to defend and protect…to slay dragons. The other half of the problem is that women condemn other women for wanting to be wives and mothers." Dottie sighed, shaking her head with discouragement. "It's a mess. It really is." She recovered quickly however and, smiling, said, "But at least you've got a dragon slayer, right?"

Cozy shook her head and exhaled a breathy laugh. "I don't *have* Jesse, as you put it, Grandma."

"But you'd like to?" Dottie suggested.

Cozy blushed. "He makes me feel…different… important and empowered…confident and comfortable…and very, very happy all the time," she confessed. "But…but…"

"But what?"

"But it's too much to hope for. He's too dreamy and flawless."

"Darling, absolutely nobody is flawless," Dottie reminded. "Though I will admit…Jesse sure is dreamy."

Dottie studied her granddaughter for a moment. She knew exactly how Cozy thought.

"You're thinking it's too good to be true," she began. "That it really couldn't be that you have actually found this wonderful man you've always dreamed of finding…and that if you have found him, he really can't possibly feel the same way about you."

Cozy shrugged.

171

"You forget who you're talking to, sweet pea," Dottie said, smiling. "This is me...me who knows you better than anyone...and that includes your mom and dad. Isn't that right?"

"Yes," Cozy admitted.

"You are special, Cozy," Dottie offered. "I know you're different than other people...that if you're feeling Jesse is the one man who could make you the happiest you could be, then you're right."

"But I'm afraid to hope," Cozy admitted. "Have you seen him, Grandma? Have you? He looks like he stepped right out of the silver screen!"

"I know," Dottie confirmed. "But don't let that be the reason you're afraid...because he's so handsome. That's worse than doubting everything if he were homely. You wouldn't lose hope in a homely boy if you felt this way, so why on earth would you lose hope because he's gorgeous? That's just plain ridiculous."

Cozy smiled—giggled as she studied her grandma for a moment—as she watched her sip her umpteenth millionth serving of cider.

"And what about you and the dashing Mr. Buckly Bryant?" Cozy asked. "Have you discovered whether or not he's a good kisser yet?"

"What do you think, love?" Dottie asked with a wink.

"And?" Cozy prodded.

"When you give me details, then I'll give you

details, sweet pea. And that's all I'm going to say…for now," her grandmother answered.

"Are Mr. Bryant's kisses as warm and moist as a summer rain, Grandma?" Cozy teased.

Dottie smiled. "Are Jesse Bryant's kisses as hot and wet as a Yellowstone hot spring, Cozy?"

Cozy laughed—wholeheartedly laughed. "Grandma! You are too funny!" She sighed as her laughter finally subsided. "Why isn't Daddy as funny as you? He is your son, after all."

"Because he takes after your Grandpa Marvin," she answered. "I loved him deeply, mind you. But he didn't have a witty bone in his body. But he was smart… really, really smart. A smart, handsome, loving, very good man." Dottie shrugged. "He just wasn't funny at all."

Cozy choked—nearly spit the cider she'd been drinking out through her nose. Oh, how she loved her grandmother—every adorable, dingy, cider-mulling, snowy-white hair on her head.

The first snowfall of the season was lovely. It had arrived in the night, silently covering the ground with a downy blanket of white. By the time the sun set the next evening, glittering frost sifted down through the night sky like tiny diamonds twinkling in the moonlight.

Jesse had asked Cozy to go for another walk with him, and she was far more than merely willing. They'd left their grandparents sitting at the kitchen table— Dottie mercilessly pouring mulled cider down Buck's throat via a Santa mug and Buck drinking every drop like the true hero that he was.

Jesse and Cozy had walked to the coffee shop and bakery and enjoyed a sugar cookie and two hot chocolates. They talked for several hours there and then stopped to build a snowman on the way home. Now they ambled arm in arm up the sidewalk toward Cozy's grandmother's house. Already the anxiety that had begun to overtake Cozy each time an evening with Jesse was about to end was threatening to taint her happiness. She tried to ignore it the best she could, but it was always there—planting doubt and insecurity in her chest.

"So Grandpa told me he kissed your grandma the other night," Jesse announced out of the blue.

"What?" she gasped, her thoughts instantly abandoning their anticipatory anxiety. "He did?"

"Yep," Jesse answered, grinning.

"And?" she pressed. "How did it go?"

Jesse shrugged. "I don't know. He didn't give me any details." He looked at her then, grinning a purely mischievous grin. "But he sure seemed happy."

"Great!" Cozy giggled. "Grandma wouldn't tell me one way or the other...the little brat."

"Well, to my way of thinking, if they're being secretive...it must be getting good."

"Really?"

Jesse nodded. "Yep. People tend to keep better secrets when things are good...especially couples, don't you think? It's like they don't want anyone infringing on their thing. Do you know what I mean?"

"I do," Cozy admitted. And she did know. She hadn't told her grandmother about the night Jesse had kissed her. It was as if she were afraid to tell anyone—as if telling someone might mean it would never happen again. Of course, it hadn't happened again. Except for the quick kiss they'd shared in the parking lot four days earlier after Jesse had rescued Cozy from the café, he hadn't kissed her again.

She tried not to worry about it—tried to imagine that he was only attempting to be a gentleman—but she did worry about it. It seemed she worried a lot lately—at least where Jesse Bryant was concerned.

They turned up the walkway and started toward the porch. Cozy's anxiety began to return. The evening was almost over—again.

"We better get you inside and get you warmed up, Little Red Riding Hood," Jesse said.

"It'll be Little Red Running Nose if we don't hurry," she said. "It's freezing out here!"

Jesse chuckled and then paused a moment, playfully frowning as he studied her. "Is every coat you own red…with a hood?" he asked, tugging at the hood of her ski jacket.

"Pretty much," she said, though she'd really never noticed it before.

He smiled, and she thought her heart might literally catch fire—just from the way he was looking at her. He was looking at her as if—as if…

Suddenly, she reached out, taking hold of his arm

and pulling him down into the bushes near the front picture window of her grandmother's house—the one that looked into the family room.

"Get down!" she ordered in a whisper.

"Why?" Jesse asked in a whisper as he crouched down beside her.

Cozy had inadvertently glanced into the front room via the picture window. She still couldn't believe she'd seen what she thought she'd seen.

"Didn't you see that?" she asked, knowing her eyes were as wide as saucers—and with good reason.

"See what?"

"You didn't see them sitting on the couch just now?" she whispered.

"No. Why?" Jesse asked. The expression of puzzlement on his face was purely adorable—if a drop-dead-gorgeous man could be termed adorable, that is.

Cozy shook her head in lingering disbelief. "Our grandparents are in there making out!" she told him.

Jesse smiled and frowned at the same time. "No way."

"Yes way!" she assured him. "I saw them…just now through the window." She shook her head again, giggling. "You'd think they'd have more decorum than that, at their age."

Jesse smiled. Reaching up and taking hold of the windowsill, he started to inch up, intending to peer through the window.

"No!" Cozy exclaimed in a whisper. "They'll see you!"

Jesse's eyebrows arched with sarcasm. "Not if they're otherwise engaged."

"Jesse!" Cozy scolded as he peered over the windowsill into her grandmother's front room.

His smile broadened. "They're not making out," he said.

"They are so," Cozy argued. Frowning—for she could tell he didn't believe her—she took hold of the windowsill and pulled herself up to peer over it and into the house. At that very moment, Buck leaned over and kissed her grandmother again. Vindication! "I told you they were making out," she whispered.

Jesse glanced to her, frowning again. "They're not making out," he argued. "They're just kissing."

Cozy looked to him, dramatizing her expression of exasperation. "Is there a difference?" she asked.

Though his brow was still puckered in a frown, Jesse exhaled a breathy chuckle and said, "Hell yes, there's a difference! Where have you been?"

Cozy playfully glared to him and then looked back to the comfortable and romantic scene inside. She smiled as she saw Buck slowly put his arm around her grandmother's shoulder and softly kiss her on the lips.

"You see?" she said. "They're totally making out! It looks like your grandpa is quite the Romeo there, Mr. Bryant."

"Oh, I'm sure he is," Jesse said. "But I'm telling you…he's just kissing her. They're nowhere near to making out."

Cozy rolled her eyes. "It's just a choice of

terminology. What's the difference, really?"

"Are you kidding me?" Jesse asked.

Cozy looked to him, her heart and stomach both leaping into her throat as she gazed into the smoldering intensity of his blue eyes.

"No," she finally managed to respond.

"You're kidding me," he repeated. "There is a world of difference between making out and just kissing, Cozy Robbins."

She giggled, sighed, "Whatever, Jesse Bryant," and returned her attention to the warm, dreamy picture of idealistic romance playing out before her.

Cozy gasped, however, as she felt Jesse take hold of the back of her coat and pull her away from the window. Before she could begin to understand what was about to transpire, she found herself flat on her back in the snow with Jesse crouching over her like a wolf who had only just forced its prey into submission. He pinned her wrists at either side of her head, holding them firmly against the ground with his powerful hands.

"That thing between us the other night," he began, "*that* was a kiss."

"I-I know that, you brat," she said. She was breathless. Not for him having gently thrown her down in the snow, but for his nearness—his predatory position—the feel of his warm breath on her face as he crouched above her.

"That was a kiss," he repeated.

Cozy gasped as his head descended toward hers.

His lips were soft against hers—tender and somewhat playful. Instantly her heart began to hammer. The ringing in her ears was like Christmas bells tolling, and she felt dizzy.

He paused, mumbling, "That was also a kiss. And this is another kiss."

Again he kissed her, coaxing her lips to part in meeting his. Though more firmly applied, this kiss was still controlled—tender and easy. Certainly Cozy had begun to tremble. Such an inferno blazed in her chest that she could hardly draw a steady breath.

Slowly—calculatingly—Jesse kissed her upper lip. Over and over he kissed it—allowing his warm lips to linger against hers each time. She was breathless as he then kissed her lower lip—gently tugged at it with such a slow and measured tempo that she thought she might melt into a puddle there in the snow.

"That's a kiss, Cozy," Jesse said. His voice was low—smooth and alluring like mulling spices.

She gasped and startled as he took hold of the front of her coat, pulling her into a sitting position. "And this," he began, still holding tight to the front of her coat, "is making out."

In one swift and powerful motion, Jesse sat back against the outer wall of the house, maneuvering Cozy to sitting in his lap. His strong arms banded around her, and Cozy's heart nearly burst from her chest as Jesse's mouth absolutely seized hers. Moist, heated, and demanding, Jesse's consuming, passionate kiss overwhelmed Cozy with not only his evident desire but her own! The thought flitted through her mind that something inside her had only just been awakened—an energy, a vigor, a pure and powerful effervescence that had been dormant before.

Jesse's five-o'clock shadow chafed the tender flesh of her chin and cheeks as his mouth ground to hers. Cozy wanted to be closer to him—to meld with him somehow—and she let her hands go around his neck, pulling herself more snuggly against him. She wished she didn't have her snow gloves on—wished she could run her fingers over the hot flesh at the back of his neck and up through his dark hair.

Almost as if he sensed her frustration, Jesse broke from her a moment. She gasped as he pulled them both to their feet, his purely predatory gaze never leaving her mesmerized one. He stripped off his snow gloves and threw them to the ground—took hold of hers and pulled them from her hands, dropping them into the snow as well.

Cozy felt her mouth begin to water as she stared at him. He unzipped his coat and reached out, unzipping hers. She stumbled as he took hold of the front of her coat, pulling her to one side of the large picture window at the front of her grandma's house.

Turning her body and pinning her back against the wall with his, Jesse took her face in his hands. His eyes were a smoldering blue, like sapphires that had somehow caught flame.

"Kiss me. Now," he growled.

Cozy had only an instant to breathe, "Okay," before his mouth captured hers again.

Weakened by desire and longing, she melted to him, allowing her arms to go around his waist. Her hands traveled from his waist up and over his back, the warmth of his body penetrating his shirt to warm her palms. Fisting the fabric of his shirt in her hands, Cozy allowed herself to revel in what was happening—to soak in the unfamiliar bliss Jesse was bathing her in. Over and over his mouth worked to somehow absorb or exhaust hers—to burn her up—to consume her with a warm and balmy fevered affection.

It was cold outside—Cozy knew it was. Yet she didn't feel the cold—only the warmth of Jesse's body as he held her to him—as their coats, unzipped and hanging open, acted as a barrier between the elements and their passion. As he continued to kiss her, the rough graze of his whiskers against the sensitive flesh around her mouth proved further titillating to her rather than uncomfortable. She could smell the faint, lingering scent of his aftershave—the spice of some masculine-scented soap or shampoo. She could smell the snow and frost in his hair, the tranquilizing aroma of wood smoke still clinging to his coat.

Slowly, the hungry nature of his kiss—the thirsty nature of hers—the feverish exchange broiling between them—settled. In a moment more, Jesse offered Cozy one last, tender, and warm kiss before releasing her.

She couldn't stop the audible sigh of blissful

satisfaction that escaped her lungs, and she blushed as Jesse smiled at her.

"I'll take that as a good sign," he teased.

Cozy bit her lip, embarrassed that she'd allowed her delight to be so obvious.

"Now that you understand the difference between kissing and making out," he began, retrieving their gloves from the snowy ground, "let's go to Grandpa's house and get you warmed up before you catch pneumonia."

Cozy smiled at him as he helped her put her gloves on and zipped up her coat. "Actually, I'm already pretty warmed up," she mumbled with blatant insinuation. She could hardly believe she'd said it, but she had, and as Jesse's smile broadened, she was glad.

Jesse chuckled and nodded with approval. "Are you just flirting with me, Cozy Robbins?" he teased. "Or are you baiting me into demonstrating the difference between kissing and making out again?"

Cozy shrugged and started toward the sidewalk. "What do you think?"

Jesse looked to her grandma's window, and she followed his gaze. Buck and her grandma were still sitting on the couch.

"I think my grandpa and your grandma are going to be occupied for a while," Jesse said, winking at her.

Cozy giggled as he lunged toward her then, taking her by the waist and lifting her up onto one shoulder as if she were no more than a sack of flour, and started down the walkway toward the sidewalk and street.

She couldn't believe how fast he was walking. Still, she felt bad, for it couldn't be an easy thing to do—carrying her down the sidewalk.

"Put me down!" she laughed, slapping him on the back. "You'll break your back!"

"Nope. And besides, you might chicken out and run home to your grandma if I put you down," he said as he increased the speed of his gait.

Cozy laughed as he hurried up the front porch of his grandpa's house and began fumbling in his front pocket. "Put me down, Jesse!" she begged. "I promise I won't run off."

"I don't trust you," he mumbled as he used his teeth to remove his glove and then returned to trying to pull his keys out of his pocket.

Cozy playfully slapped him on the back again as she heard the front door to Buck Bryant's house open. "Brrr!" he shivered, setting her feet on the floor at last. "Okay," he began, stripping off his coat. "You make the hot chocolate…and I'll start the fire and get the chestnuts ready."

"What?" Cozy asked, amused and fascinated by the expression of mischief on his face.

"I'll get the fire started so we can warm up and roast a few chestnuts," he reiterated. "You make us some hot chocolate, and then we'll settle down on the couch for a little…light conversation."

"I think we've had quite enough 'light conversation' for one night, don't you?" she asked—desperately hoping he would disagree.

He frowned and feigned thoughtfulness for a moment. "Um…no," he said, taking hold of her chin and pressing a smoldering, alluring kiss to her mouth. "If our grandparents can sit on the couch and make out in front of the fire…then so can we."

"But you said they were just kissing," Cozy reminded him.

"Cozy, Cozy, Cozy," he said, his voice low and alluring. "Haven't you learned your lesson yet? Wolves are very good hunters, baby. I only said that so I could throw you down in the snow and taste your mouth. When are you ever going to learn?"

"Never…if I'm lucky," she breathed.

Cozy sighed then as Jesse gathered her into his arms, growled like a wolf, and laid claim to her lips.

CHAPTER NINE

November waned. The brilliant golden leaves of the autumn cottonwoods had disappeared with the first snow. Although Cozy always missed the leaves when they were gone, she loved the delicate frost feathers of December that decorated the window glass each night. In truth, Cozy found herself loving everything—the cool winter air, not having to go to the café every day, her family, and the way her grandmother had traded in her mulling spices for almond extract in order to keep her warm, orange almond punch simmering and ever ready on her stovetop. Yet for everything Cozy found to love in December—including the delicious anticipation of Christmas—what she loved most, and more than anything else, was Jesse Bryant.

Cozy had never been a pessimist—never. She'd always seen the hopeful and bright side of things. Yet she found herself waiting for a conflict—for something that would pull Jesse away from her. It all seemed too good to be true—too wonderful to be real. Even the growing romance between her grandmother and Buck made her nervous somehow. Her grandmother was so happy—happier than Cozy could remember her having been in years. Nothing seemed to distract Buck from Dottie or Dottie from Buck. Mr. Bryant even took to drinking her grandma's orange almond punch as voraciously as he'd consumed the gallons and gallons of mulled cider. Still, Cozy struggled to believe it all really was as beautiful and untainted as it appeared—especially her relationship with Jesse.

Furthermore, the longer she and Jesse were involved, the more Cozy knew she could never give him up—never! At least not without being forever scarred—her heart permanently maimed. She'd spoken with her grandma about it, of course—and as always, Dottie Robbins was the perfect feel-good fairy.

"Darling, you've just seen too many movies and read too many mystery novels," Dottie had told Cozy. "In real life, things really work out...and much more smoothly than they do in fiction. Don't worry so much, pumpkin. Your forehead will wrinkle prematurely if you do."

Cozy always felt better after a pep talk from her grandmother. She wondered how it was that her grandma seemed so free of anxiety all the time. Perhaps it was simply age and experience, for Dottie always said that ninety percent of everything people worried over never even actually transpired. Or perhaps it was simply that she'd learned to mask her concerns better than Cozy had. Whatever the reason, Cozy had long before determined that when she was in her sixties, she wanted to emulate Dottie's character, nature, and happy countenance. Thus, she knew she had to master it soon—and she tried.

Still, the anticipation of some sort of something that would disturb her mounting relationship with Jesse pricked at her brain, like a goathead thorn stuck in her sock. Even so, she did her best to ignore it—to simply bathe in the wonder of loving Jesse Bryant and knowing he cared deeply for her. Neither of them had actually spoken the three little magic words out loud to one another, but Cozy knew she loved Jesse—and she knew he at least owned intense feelings toward her. That fact was never more evident than the first time Jesse took her to his own house.

This time it was Buck and Dottie that had gone for a stroll down to the coffee house and bakery on the corner. As Cozy sat with Jesse on her grandmother's sofa—nestled warmly against him with his arm around her shoulders—they watched the candle flames flickering in the crackle-glass votives on the mantel. Her grandmother's walnut-ornament-adorned Christmas tree stood in one corner of the room, and the fire in the fireplace provided the only other lighting. It was a soft, serene, and very romantic atmosphere.

Cozy sighed with contentment, thinking that moment was one of the most wonderful she'd ever known.

"Your grandma's tree is really something," Jesse noted.

Cozy smiled. "Oh, yes! She takes great care when decorating it. See how she makes sure every one of the hinged walnuts is displayed just so?"

Jesse chuckled. "Yeah. Mine looks like that little bald cartoon kid picked it out and decorated it."

Cozy giggled, sat up, and looked at him. "I still don't know if I even believe you have a tree," she teased him. It was true, for she just couldn't seem to imagine Jesse Bryant—being a bachelor and living alone—putting up a Christmas tree and decorating it.

"I told you I have one," he said, smiling at her.

Cozy's eyes narrowed with suspicion. "I think you just bought my ornaments because you felt pressured into it by my grandma."

"Nope," he assured her. "I really wanted them. They're on my tree right this minute."

"No, they are not," she said, playfully slapping him on his granite-hard chest.

"They are too!" he assured her with a chuckle.

"I still don't believe you," she said, snuggling up against him once more.

"Well, they are," he said. "Though...I am thinking that some of those candle things your grandma always has on her mantel would really perk my place up a bit."

Cozy sat up again. "I have a ton of them!" she exclaimed. "You can borrow some of mine! They're just sitting in boxes in my room at home."

"Would you think that was too girlie of me?" he asked, his expression entirely serious. "To have candles on my mantel at home?"

"Of course not!" she assured him. "Every home

should have candles on the mantel...especially at Christmas."

"Even a guy's mantel?" he asked, still uncertain. "I mean, it could be construed as...you know...weird."

"Your grandpa has candles on his mantel," she reminded him.

"Yeah," he chuckled. "Those cheap ones you get at the grocery store, and they're just sitting on old mismatched saucers. They're nothing like those," he said, motioning to the crackle glass. He frowned, thoughtful for a moment. "Do you have any that aren't so...um...feminine? Your grandma's all have, like, little birds and stuff. I don't know if I could—"

"I have some with pinecones and fir branches," Cozy interjected. "And what's more masculine than pinecones and fir branches? That's totally woodsy...a guy sort of thing."

Jesse's eyebrows arched as he considered what she'd suggested. "So, if I drive you over to your house and we pick up these masculine glass candle things...do you want to come over to my house and slap them up on my mantel for me?"

Cozy's heart nearly leapt out of her mouth. He was going to take her to his house? She'd wanted to see where he lived since the moment she met him. But he spent every evening with his grandfather, her grandmother, and her, so the opportunity never presented itself before.

"I would love it!" she exclaimed, entirely unable to hide her excitement. "Only, one *arranges* candle votives on a mantel. One does not slap them up."

He smiled, laughed, and kissed her forehead. "You're such a girl, Cozy Robbins," he sighed. "Come on then. Let's go."

"Shouldn't we wait for Grandma and Buck?" she asked.

"We'll leave a note on the kitchen table," he answered. "I heard your grandma tell Grandpa she was taking her keys, just in case you and I had to go home before they got back."

"Okay, then," Cozy said, fairly leaping to her feet. "Let's go make your mantel more Christmas-y, Mr. Bryant."

He stood, taking her hand as he led her toward the kitchen. "If you're a good Little Red Riding Hood," he began, "I just might let you sample my first batch of raspberry almonds for the year."

"Ooo!" Cozy teased, shivering with exaggerated anticipation. "So you're saying my life will be changed forever tonight?"

Jesse paused a moment before answering, wildly amused at the innocent way Cozy had of saying something he could easily turn into an insinuation. Still, he decided to let her off the hook this time. After all, he wasn't certain yet; he wasn't certain she was ready for him to forever change her life the way he really wanted to.

"Oh, yes," he answered. "Once you've tasted my raspberry almonds...you'll be completely helpless to resist me."

"Well, that's not really anything new, is it?" she flirted.

"Ooo! Little Red!" he growled, pulling her into his arms. "Don't you know better than to tempt the wolf?"

She smiled, and he couldn't keep from kissing her. And it was no gentle and tender kiss he enforced. Rather it was a heated, driven, all-consuming kiss that he well knew took her breath away. She didn't shrink from it in the least, however, but met his mouth with pure as much desire, fiery wanting, and passion as he vigorously applied to hers.

He could've lingered forever in kissing her—had to fight to keep from tossing her over one shoulder, carrying her into the privacy of the den, and...

"Let's get that note written so we can go," he said, abruptly breaking the seal of their mouths.

"Okay," she sighed, smiling at him with such glistening emotion in her eyes that he almost dropped to his knees then and there and proposed marriage.

"Good," he said instead, however. "It's high time I proved to you that I bought your walnut things for my Christmas tree."

"Yes, it is," Cozy agreed, releasing him and going to retrieve a pen and paper from her grandmother's junk drawer.

"Wonderful!" Buck exclaimed once Dottie had finished reading Cozy's note. "He's taking her to his place? This is big, Dottie. Real big."

"How big?" Dottie asked as mounting excitement

caused her heart to start hammering.

Buck nodded, his smile broadening. "Big enough that...well, I don't want to jinx anything."

"How big, Buck?" Dottie whined. She was almost miserable with anticipation.

"He's letting her in...letting her past the last blockade he's built up around himself," Buck answered. "Jesse guards his privacy like a rottweiler. He never takes a woman to his home. He always said he never would...not until he found the one that was going to live in it with him."

Dottie squealed and began bounding up and down with euphoric delight. Giggling with joy, she threw her arms around Buck's neck.

"Oh, Buck. I knew it! I knew they were just meant for each other," she squealed. "I knew it from the moment I saw them in the same room!"

Buck chuckled. "Me, too, sugar cube," he said. "But they still have a ways to go yet. We need to be patient."

"Oh, I know. I do know," Dottie said, releasing him and smoothing her hair. She was sure he thought she was a complete idiot for acting so childish, but she hadn't been able to help it. Cozy was going to know every happiness with Jesse—Dottie was sure of it. "But I really do feel as if...oh, Buck! Can you even imagine how wonderful their lives would be together?"

Buck smiled, reached out, and took Dottie in his arms.

"I imagine they'll be about as happy as ours will," he said.

He chuckled when her eyebrows puckered into a puzzled frown. "What?'" she asked.

"As soon as these kids finally get their act together—as soon as we're sure they don't need any more urging from us—I want you to marry me, Dottie Robbins," he said.

Dottie gasped, moisture instantly filling her beautiful blue eyes. "Really?" she squeaked. She began to tremble in his arms, and tears began rolling down her cheeks.

"Really," Buck confirmed. "You know I love you, Dottie. You're unlike any woman I've ever known." He paused to tenderly brush the tears from her face with the back of his hand. "Let's live out our lives together—laugh, be happy, and love like we never imagined we would again…maybe even differently than we did before." She nodded, still weeping and unable to speak. "Though, if you keep pouring cider and punch down my gullet, you're gonna drown me before I have a chance to marry you and carry you away on wings of passion."

She laughed through her tears. "All right," she sniffled. "For wings of passion with you…I'll neglect my mulling cider and orange almond punch more often." She started crying again and buried her face in her hands, and he gathered her into his arms.

"What're you crying for, honey?" he chuckled.

"I never thought…that day Cozy and I were spying

on you and Jesse through the kitchen window...I never dared to imagine this! I never, never dared even dream of it," she cried.

"You never dared to dream of it?" Buck asked with amused skepticism.

Dottie raised her head once more, sniffled, and brushed tears from her cheeks. "Well, maybe I did dream of it...a little."

"I love you, Dottie," Buck sighed, taking her face in his hands.

Dottie gazed at the man who had captured her heart—at the man she had fallen so desperately in love with—at the hero who made her feel seventeen all over again. "I love you, Buck," she said. "Oh, how I love you!"

"Then come here," he said, pulling her into his arms again. "Come here and let me kiss you the way Jesse kisses Cozy."

Dottie giggled, her heart so filled with love she thought it might actually burst. "Are you sure you know how?" she teased, wrapping her arms around his neck.

Buck chuckled. "I taught that boy everything he knows, honey. And I do mean everything."

As Buckly Bryant kissed her, tears streamed over Dottie Robbins's cheeks. Buck's lips were warm and moist, his mouth laced with impassioned love and desire as he kissed her—kissed her as she hadn't been kissed in seemingly decades. Feelings and sensations she thought were lost long ago blossomed like the earliest flowers of spring as he awakened them within her. In those moments, as she allowed herself to drown in physical passion and heart-pounding love, Dottie knew she must be the happiest woman on the face of the earth.

And there was more—more that flittered through her mind as Buck continued to rain bliss over her—Cozy. Dottie knew that if she were this happy—this euphoric in Buck's arms—then how perfectly blissful would Cozy be in Jesse's?

She sighed as Buck broke the seal of their lips a moment to gaze into her eyes.

"I owe finding you to Jesse, you know," he told her. "It was Jesse that talked me into moving down here. It was Jesse who found the house next door and did everything to get me to buy it."

Dottie smiled. "It's ironic, isn't it?" she whispered, reaching up to run her fingers through his soft, silver hair.

"What is?" he asked, kissing the tip of her nose.

"That all this time…all this time that they've been trying to make certain you and I ended up like this… they've never once caught on to our involvement in making certain they didn't miss falling in love," she said.

Buck chuckled. "Yep," he agreed. "But that was only because they're such good kids…and because, whether they've admitted it or not, we were their excuse to spend time together."

Dottie nodded and twisted a lock of Buck's hair around her index finger as she gazed into the mesmerizing blue of his eyes. "I do love you, Buckly Bryant. So very, very much."

Buck smiled. "Then prove it, honey."

Dottie giggled as his head descended toward hers once more, and as her lips felt the first touch of his, she knew it—she knew her heart would be forever seventeen and in love!

❧

"Jesse!" Cozy breathed as Jesse opened the passenger's side door of his truck. She was so overwhelmed by the lighting display of his house and the trees in his yard that she stumbled as she climbed down. "Oh, Jesse, it's breathtaking! It's literally breathtaking."

Jesse shrugged as if the huge cottonwood tree entirely drenched in white icicle lights and looking like something out of a fantasy were nothing out of the ordinary.

"I think it looked a little better last year," he said, frowning as he studied the tree for a moment. "I'm not quite sure what I did different…but something seems a little off."

Cozy looked at him with her mouth gaping open in astonishment. "Are you serious?" she asked, returning her attention to the lighting display. "It's… it's like nothing I've ever seen before!" And it was true. Not only was the little, cozy-looking two-story house dripping with perfectly arranged white icicle lights, the tree was awe-inspiring! There was also a waterfall, pond, and deer scene on the front lawn similar to the one Jesse had created for her grandmother—only this scene was vastly more detailed! The blue lights creating the waterfall blinked, flashed, and twinkled in such a perfect way that it appeared as if water were truly cascading down and into a pond. There were also five animated deer instead of three, and every tree and bush in the yard was flawlessly decorated with tiny white lights so that a person could almost swear they'd stepped into some sort of fantastical winter dream.

"Jesse!" she breathed, looking at him again. He was still studying the large cottonwood, an expression of frustrated dissatisfaction on his face. "Jesse…it's…I can't even think of the words!"

"Thanks," he mumbled, still studying the big tree to one side of the yard.

Cozy held her breath then, not quite sure she should believe what she was hearing. "Is that music?" she asked as further astonishment rinsed her body with goose bumps.

"Mm hm," he said—as if hearing Mannheim Steamroller's beautiful version of "Silent Night" wafting out over the night air were the most natural thing in the world. "I just pipe it out through the… okay, that's really bugging me," he said, starting toward the cottonwood.

Cozy caught hold of his arm, however. When he looked at her, he seemed puzzled by the tears in her eyes.

"What's the matter, baby?" he asked, taking her face between his hands.

"Who are you?" she asked, smiling at him.

He seemed to understand then. Shrugging his broad, broad shoulders, he answered, "Just an electrician who likes to slap up a few Christmas lights here and there." He kissed her and then put his arm around her shoulders. "Come on. But be prepared, Little Red… 'cause the inside ain't nothing like the outside."

"Well, you wouldn't need my crackle-glass votive if it were, now would you?" she said, brushing a tear from her cheek.

"Oh, yeah! I almost forgot to bring them in. Wait here a minute," he said, turning and hurrying back to his truck.

Cozy shook her head, still unable to believe the breathtaking beauty Jesse had created. "He's unreal!" she whispered.

"Here," he said as he returned, carrying the box of crackle glass they'd retrieved from her home. "Let's get inside. It's freaking cold out here tonight!"

"Yeah…it is," Cozy breathed, shaking her head in residual awe as they walked beneath the cottonwood tree dripping with white lights.

The moment she stepped into Jesse's house, she could smell it—the rich, sweet scent of raspberry. "It smells wonderful in here," she said as he closed the door behind them.

"Only at this time of year," he chuckled.

He turned on the light, and Cozy smiled—bit her

lip to keep from giggling with delight. Jesse was right: the inside of his house looked absolutely nothing like the outside of it. It was purely masculine, void of any softening decorative embellishments. It was a beautiful house, but it wasn't homey—not in the least. No wonder Jesse loved spending time at her grandmother's. She thought it was amazing—the stark contrast to the beautiful, inviting scene outside.

She did giggle a little then when her attention fell to the Christmas tree in one corner.

"You see? I told you I had a tree," he said triumphantly.

Cozy bit her tongue, determined to not agree with him that his tree looked like the well-known little bald cartoon kid picked it out and decorated it—even though it appeared exactly like he had.

"You certainly do," she said, still smiling. "I stand corrected, Mr. Bryant."

"Come on. I'll let you see your walnuts too," he said, taking her hand and leading her toward his tree. He leaned down and pressed the reset button on a power strip, and the pitiful tree burst to life. Cozy did note that the lights were perfect. There were tons and tons of them, and she thought the lights alone saved the thing from being downright ugly.

"See? There they are," he said proudly, pointing to the five walnut ornaments clustered together in the middle of the tree. Cozy giggled as she reached out and opened one of the hinged ornaments. Other than a few colored glass ornaments strewn here and there, Cozy's walnut ornaments were the only ones on the tree. "Do you like it?" he asked.

Cozy smiled, wondering how in the world the man could've created the wonderment outside but have such a ghastly looking Christmas tree. "It's beautiful," she said—and she meant it. It was beautiful, after all. For all its pitiful imperfection, Jesse's Christmas tree was absolutely beautiful—beautiful because it was so awful!

Cozy threw her arms around Jesse's neck and held tight to him. She could never have loved a man who could decorate a Christmas tree better than she could. To her, Jesse's hideous tree only added to his heroic character.

"It's that bad, huh?" he laughed as he kissed her neck and tightly held her to him.

Cozy giggled, but she would never admit to him that his tree was pathetic. "You are adorable!" she said instead. "How do you do it?"

"Do what? Mess up a perfectly good tree?" he asked.

Cozy pulled away from him just enough to be able to gaze into his eyes. "No. How do you just keep getting more wonderful with every day that goes by?"

"Okay…what do you want?" he teased.

"Well, first of all," she began, pulling herself from his arms and taking her cell phone out of her pocket, "I need a picture of this tree. I'm thinking of doing a website for my ornaments, and this will be perfect for the—"

"How not to decorate with Cozy Robbins's walnut things?" he finished for her.

Cozy giggled, steadied her phone, and snapped a digital image of Jesse's tree. "You are my hero, Jesse," she sighed.

"Because my tree is so bad?" he asked.

"There are too many reasons to list," she said, smiling at him

"Hmm," he mumbled skeptically. "Well, let's unpack these candle things and light them up so your attention won't be on that tree all night long."

Cozy sighed as she took one last look at Jesse's sad, yet wonderfully lit, Christmas tree. She loved him all the more for it. She loved him. And no matter what conflict arose to try and strip him from her, she was determined that nothing ever could.

❦

"Okay," Jesse said, returning from the kitchen and plopping down on the sofa next to Cozy. "Are you ready for me to change your life, Cozy Robbins?" He held a brown paper lunch sack in one hand, and Cozy could smell raspberry and almond.

The room was warm and comfortable. The fire in the fireplace crackled and spit with the soothing sounds and scents that only burning wood could provide. Tiny flames flickered inside the crackle-glass votives Cozy had lovingly arranged on Jesse's hearth.

She gazed at Jesse for a moment before answering, thinking that he already had changed her life. She knew she would never be the same again—not after knowing him—not after loving him—not after the way his kisses made her feel.

"I'm ready," she said at last.

He smiled, pure mischief glistening in his eyes. "Okay then…have at it," he said, offering the brown paper lunch sack to her.

"I still can't believe you're such an experienced chef," she teased him as she accepted the bag.

He shrugged. "Jerky and raspberry almonds," he said. "They're the only two things I can cook without a microwave." He paused, adding, "Other than grilling meat on an outdoor grill."

Cozy opened the paper sack and peered inside. The almonds inside were coated in what appeared to be powdered sugar. "Mmm!" she hummed as the scent of raspberry filled her lungs. "They smell good!"

"They are good," Jesse said. "Go on. Try one. But I promise you…once you start, you won't be able to stop."

She smiled at him. "You're very confident where your raspberry almonds are concerned."

"Yep."

Reaching into the bag, Cozy chose an almond. She started to put it in her mouth, but Jesse reached out, taking hold of her wrist and stalling her.

"I should warn you, Little Red," he began, "once you go down this path…there's no going back. These almonds really will change your life. I promise you that."

"Why?" she asked then. "Why are these going to change my life? I can't think of anything edible that would change anybody's life."

"Well, for one thing...I've mixed in a little love potion stuff," he said. "You know...to make you fall in love with me."

Cozy's smile faded a little as her amusement turned quickly to nervous anticipation. "A love potion, huh?"

"Yep," Jesse confirmed with a nod. "After you eat even one of those almonds, you won't be able to resist me. You'll fall helplessly in love with me...and then I can do whatever I want with you."

"That sounds like a very wolfish thing to do," she teased.

"Maybe," he said. "But I've got to find some way to have you...now don't I? After all, I've been hunting you for a month now. So try this almond, and fall in love with me, Cozy." He kissed the back of her hand and released her wrist.

"Wh-what if I'm already in love with you?" she bravely ventured.

He smiled, and she knew he was pleased. "Then the almonds will just help you to say it." He winked at her. "Go on, baby. Eat one."

Cozy was trembling with excitement and delight. Was this his way of confessing he loved her? Whether he was just being playful or was truly trying to tell her something, she did know he wanted her to taste the almonds he was so very proud of. She knew it was important to him—that they represented more than just something good to eat—that they were part of his past and who he was.

Therefore, Cozy raised the almond to her mouth—

bit into it. Instantly such an explosion of delight filled her mouth that she actually wondered for a moment if there was some magic ingredient in the almond. She truly had never tasted anything so delicious—not in all her life! She put the rest of the almond in her mouth and immediately reached into the paper bag for another. Surely she was imagining how scrumptious they were. But after she ate a second almond—a third and then a fourth—she still knew that Jesse's raspberry almonds were the most delicious thing she'd ever eaten.

"Oh my gosh!" she exclaimed at last. "Jesse, I can't believe how good they are!"

He smiled, obviously pleased and amused by her reaction. "I told you," he said. "Once again, you doubted me...even though I promised you they would change your life."

"Oh my gosh!" she breathed again, popping two almonds at once into her mouth. "Jesse, seriously. I have never tasted anything like this!"

"So is it working then?" he asked.

"What?" Cozy mumbled with her mouth full.

"The love potion in them," he answered. "Are you in love with me yet?"

Cozy swallowed the nuts she'd been chewing—began to tremble with anticipation again. "I was in love with you long before this," she confessed.

She heard him exhale a heavy sigh—a sigh of relief. Leaning closer to her, she looked up into his eyes as she felt his hand slip beneath her hair to caress the back of her neck. His expression was that of contentment and happiness—mingled with desire.

He kissed her—tenderly at first, the way he had the very first time they'd kissed. His lips were warm and tempting.

"I love you," he said. The low, provocative tone of his voice that Cozy loved so much did something to her—broke a chain that had been holding her back—and she dropped the bag of almonds, throwing her arms around his neck and kissing him, open-mouthed and with consuming ferocity!

Jesse didn't pause but rather gathered her into his arms, returning her kiss with a ravenous hunger. Cozy could feel it then—the passion and desire threatening to devour them both—to exhaust their self-control. She felt his body trembling as violently as hers did, and she feared that her strength to resist him would fail her.

Suddenly, however, Jesse broke the seal of their kiss, pulling her tightly against him and holding her as the rough whiskers of his chin deliciously scratched at her neck.

"I-I'm sorry my house is so...so plain," he breathed. "I-I'm not much with...with stuff like that."

Cozy understood that he was trying to distract them—trying to cool the passion that threatened to whirl them out of control.

"It's fine," she breathed, caressing the back of his neck with one hand as her other was lost in the softness of his dark hair. "It just needs a woman's touch."

He released her then, pulling away from her, taking

her chin in his hand, and gazing into her eyes. "Will you be the woman to touch it, Cozy?" he asked.

"What?" she breathed. Her mind was still fuzzy from the effects of his kiss, and she didn't know what he meant.

"Will you put your woman's touch to this house... and to me?" he mumbled. His eyes were smoldering with emotion—filled with sincerity. "I want you to take another walk with me, Cozy Robbins," Jesse breathed.

"Now?" Cozy asked, afraid to believe that what she was beginning to think he was saying was actually what he was saying. "But it's so late...and really cold out and..."

Jesse grinned and caressed her lips with his thumb. "I want you to take another walk with me, Cozy...one that will never end. I want you to walk through life with me...through forever with me, Cozy. I want you to marry me."

Tears spilled from her eyes—raced over her cheeks.

"But...but this was all about Grandma...and Buck," she breathed.

Jesse shook his head. "This was all about you and me, Cozy. It always was. They just got lucky and fell in love while they were watching us do the same thing."

More tears streamed from Cozy's eyes. "But you've only known me a month," she said. "How can you love me after only a month?"

"How can you love me after only a month?" he asked her.

She shook her head, afraid to believe he had truly

asked her to marry him. "But there...there has to be something else...some conflict. An old girlfriend who's obsessed with you...or something. It can't be that you just met me and—"

"There's no conflict, Cozy," he said. "Sometimes people really do just fall in love and live happily ever after." He kissed her then. "Live happily ever after with me, Little Red Riding Hood. Marry me and live happily ever after with me. Love me, sleep in my arms...let me share your bed and show you how passionate a wolf really can be."

Cozy giggled a little through her tears. "You are rather wolfish, you know," she whispered. "Leading me in here under the pretense of showing me that pitiful Christmas tree."

Jesse chuckled and kissed her again. "Oh, I'm more wolfish than you know, baby," he said. "I meant to have you eat that whole bag of nuts before I proposed to you...but I couldn't hold off any longer."

"Why? So I'd be overcome by your love potion?" she breathed.

Jesse retrieved the bag from where Cozy had dropped it. "Here," he said, offering it to her again. "Dig down a little deeper in there."

Cozy's heart began to hammer more furiously than it had been hammering even a moment before. Tentatively, she reached into the bag of roasted and flavored raspberry almonds, gasping when she felt something square and solid in the bottom.

Carefully and with a trembling hand, she removed

the red-velvet-covered jewelry box protected by a plastic sandwich bag. "I have to be dreaming," she stammered breathlessly.

"You're not dreaming," Jesse assured her. "But you still haven't told me if you'll take that long walk with me, baby."

"Of course!" Cozy cried. "Of course! Right this minute if you want!"

Jesse smiled, sighing with relief as if he'd been holding his breath. "Thank you," he breathed. "There for a minute I thought I was going to have the ugliest Christmas tree in town for the rest of my life."

Cozy giggled through her tears, flung her arms around his neck, and kissed him. "I love you, Jesse," she wept. "I love you more than I love life itself!"

"I love you," he said, kissing her. "More." He kissed her again, and Cozy melted at the sense of his hot, moist mouth to hers. He ended the kiss far sooner than she would have preferred, however.

"Now open it," he said, taking hold of her wrist and nodding to the sandwich-bag-covered jewelry box. "You might change your mind after you see what's inside."

"I would never change my mind, Jesse Bryant," she said.

"Open it," he said, smiling at her, brushing the tears from her cheek.

With trembling hands, Cozy Robbins removed the red velvet jewelry box from the plastic sandwich bag. Her tears and trembling increased for a moment as the thought struck her of how perfectly masculine it was to put a jewelry box in a plastic sandwich bag.

When at last she was finally able to steady her hands enough to open the red velvet box, she gasped, bursting into tears as she saw one half of a walnut shell inside—the most beautiful diamond solitaire ring she had ever seen nestled inside it.

"You like it, don't you?" Jesse asked. Cozy looked up to see him smiling with pride. "I thought it was pretty clever too," he added.

Cozy watched as Jesse removed the ring from the walnut and box, slipping it onto her left ring finger. "Take a walk with me, Cozy," he said, brushing more tears from her cheeks. "Take a walk with me, and live happily ever after."

"Okay," she breathed, trembling as Jesse kissed her.

He paused a moment, gazing lovingly into her eyes. "See? I told you those raspberry almonds would change your life…didn't I?"

"You did," she said, smiling at him

"Now kiss me, Little Red," he mumbled against her mouth.

Jesse growled, and Cozy smiled as his mouth sealed the truth—that their walks together would go on forever.

My everlasting admiration, gratitude and love…
To my husband, Kevin…
My inspiration…
My heart's desire…
The man of my every dream!

ABOUT THE AUTHOR

Marcia Lynn McClure's intoxicating succession of novels, novellas, and e-books—including *The Visions of Ransom Lake*, *A Crimson Frost*, *The Rogue Knight*, and most recently *The Pirate Ruse*—has established her as one of the most favored and engaging authors of true romance. Her unprecedented forte in weaving captivating stories of western, medieval, regency, and contemporary amour void of brusque intimacy has earned her the title "The Queen of Kissing."

Marcia, who was born in Albuquerque, New Mexico, has spent her life intrigued with people, history, love, and romance. A wife, mother, grandmother, family historian, poet, and author, Marcia Lynn McClure spins her tales of splendor for the sake of offering respite through the beauty, mirth, and delight of a worthwhile and wonderful story.

BIBLIOGRAPHY

A Better Reason to Fall in Love
A Crimson Frost
An Old-Fashioned Romance
Beneath the Honeysuckle Vine
Born for Thorton's Sake
Daydreams
Desert Fire
Divine Deception
Dusty Britches
Kiss in the Dark
Kissing Cousins
Love Me
Saphyre Snow
Shackles of Honor
Sudden Storms
Sweet Cherry Ray
Take a Walk with Me
The Anthology of Premiere Novellas Romantic Vignettes
The Fragrance of her Name
The Heavenly Surrender
The Heavenly Surrender 10th Anniversary Special Edition
The Heavenly Surrender Hardcover Edition
The Highwayman of Tanglewood
The Highwayman of Tanglewood Hardcover Edition
The Light of the Lovers' Moon
The Pirate Ruse
The Prairie Prince
The Rogue Knight
The Tide of the Mermaid Tears
The Time of Aspen Falls
The Touch of Sage

The Trove of the Passion Room
The Visions of Ransom Lake
The Whispered Kiss
The Windswept Flame
To Echo the Past
Weathered Too Young

A Better Reason to Fall in Love
Contemporary Romance

"Boom chicka wow wow!" Emmy whispered.

"Absolutely!" Tabby breathed as she watched Jagger Brodie saunter past.

She envied Jocelyn for a moment, knowing he was most likely on his way to drop something off on Jocelyn's desk—or to speak with her. Jocelyn got to talk with Jagger almost every day, whereas Tabby was lucky if he dropped graphics changes off to her once a week.

"Ba boom chicka wow wow!" Emmy whispered again. "He's sporting a red tie today! Ooo! The power tie! He must be feeling confident."

Tabby smiled, amused and yet simultaneously amazed at Emmy's observation. She'd noticed the red tie, too. "There's a big marketing meeting this afternoon," she told Emmy. "I heard he's presenting some hard-nose material."

"Then that explains it," Emmy said, smiling. "Mr. Brodie's about to rock the company's world!"

"He already rocks mine...every time he walks by," Tabby whispered.

A Crimson Frost
Historical Romance

Beloved of her father, King Dacian, and adored by her people, the Scarlet Princess Monet endeavored to serve her kingdom well—for the people of the Kingdom of Karvana were good and worthy of service. Long Monet had known that even her marriage would serve her people. Her husband would be chosen for her—for this was the way of royal existence.

Still, as any woman does—peasant or princess—Monet dreamt of owning true love—of owning choice in love. Thus, each time the raven-haired, sapphire-eyed, Crimson Knight of Karvana rode near, Monet knew regret—for in secret, she loved him—and she could not choose him.

As an arrogant king from another kingdom began to wage war against Karvana, Karvana's king, knights, and soldiers answered the challenge. The Princess Monet would also know battle. As the Crimson Knight battled with armor and blade—so the Scarlet Princess would battle in sacrifice and with secrets held. Thus, when the charge was given to preserve the heart of Karvana—Monet endeavored to serve her kingdom and forget her secreted love. Yet love is not so easily forgotten…

An Old-Fashioned Romance
Contemporary Romance

Life went along simply, if not rather monotonously, for Breck McCall. Her job was satisfying, she had true friends. But she felt empty—as if party of her soul was detached and lost to her. She longed for something—something which seemed to be missing.

Yet, there were moments when Breck felt she might almost touch something wonderful. And most of those moments came while in the presence of her handsome, yet seemingly haunted boss—Reese Thatcher.

Beneath the Honeysuckle Vine
Historical Romance

Civil War—no one could flee from the nightmare of battle and the countless lives it devoured. Everyone had sacrificed—suffered profound misery and unimaginable loss. Vivianna Bartholomew was no exception. The war had torn her from her home—orphaned her. The merciless war seemed to take everything—even the man she loved. Still, Vivianna yet knew gratitude—for a kind friend had taken her in upon the death of her parents. Thus, she was cared for—even loved.

Yet as General Lee surrendered, signaling the war's imminent end—as Vivianna remained with the remnants of the Turner family—her soul clung to the letters written by her lost soldier—to his memory written in her heart. Could a woman ever heal from the loss of such a love? Could a woman's heart forget that it may find another? Vivianna Bartholomew thought not.

Still, it is often in the world that miracles occur—that love endures even after hope has been abandoned. Thus, one balmy Alabama morning—as two ragged soldiers wound the road toward the Turner house—Vivianna began to know—to know that miracles do exist—that love is never truly lost.

Born for Thorton's Sake
Historical Romance

Maria Castillo Holt...the only daughter of a

valiant Lord and his Spanish beauty. Following the tragic deaths of her parents, Maria would find herself spirited away by conniving kindred in an endurance of neglect and misery.

However, rescued at the age of thirteen by Brockton Thorton, the son of her father's devoted friend Lord Richard Thorton, Maria would at last find blessed reprieve. Further Brockton Thorton became, from that day forth, ever the absolute center of Maria's very existence. And as the blessed day of her sixteenth birthday dawned, Maria's dreams of owning her heart's desire seemed to become a blissful reality.

Yet a fiendish plotting intruded, and Maria's hopes of realized dreams were locked away within dark, impenetrable walls. Would Maria's dreams of life with the handsome and coveted Brockton Thorton die at the hands of a demon strength?

Daydreams
Contemporary Romance

Sayler Christy knew chances were slim to none that any of her silly little daydreams would ever actually come true—especially any daydreams involving Mr. Booker, the new patient—the handsome, older patient convalescing in her grandfather's rehabilitation center.

Yet, working as a candy striper at Rawlings Rehab, Sayler couldn't help but dream of belonging to Mr. Booker—and Mr. Booker stole her heart—perhaps unintentionally—but with very little effort. Gorgeous, older, and entirely unobtainable—Sayler knew Mr.

Booker would unknowingly enslave her heart for many years to come—for daydreams were nothing more than a cruel joke inflicted by life. All dreams—daydreams or otherwise—never came true. Did they?

Desert Fire
Historical Romance

She opened her eyes and beheld, for the first time, the face of Jackson McCall. Ruggedly handsome and her noble rescuer, he would, she knew in that moment, forever hold captive her heart as he then held her life in his protective arms.

Yet she was a nameless beauty, haunted by wisps of visions of the past. How could she ever hope he would return the passionate, devotional love she secreted for him when her very existence was a riddle?

Would Jackson McCall (handsome, fascinating, brooding) ever see her as anything more than a foundling—a burden to himself and his family? And with no memory of her own identity, how then could she release him from his apparent affliction of being her protector?

Divine Deception
Historical Romance

Life experience had harshly turned its cruel countenance on the young Fallon Ashby. Her father deceased and her mother suffering with a fatal disease, Fallon was given over to her uncle, Charles Ashby, until she would reach the age of independence.

Abused, neglected, and disheartened, Fallon found herself suddenly blessed with unexpected liberation at the hand of the mysterious Trader Donavon. A wealthy landowner and respected denizen of the town, Trader Donavon concealed his feature of face within the shadows of a black cowl.

When Fallon's secretive deliverer offered two choices of true escape from her uncle, her captive heart chose its own path. Thus, Fallon married the enormous structure of mortal man—without having seen the horrid secret he hid beneath an ominous hood.

But the malicious Charles Ashby, intent on avenging his own losses at Trader Donavon's hand, set out to destroy the husband that Fallon herself held secrets concerning. Would her wicked uncle succeed and perhaps annihilate the man that his niece secretly loved above all else?

Dusty Britches
Historical Romance

Angelina Hunter was seriously minded, and it was a good thing. Her father's ranch needed a woman who could endure the strenuous work of ranch life. Since her mother's death, Angelina had been that woman. She had no time for frivolity—no time for a less severe side of life. Not when there was so much to be done—hired hands to feed, a widower father to care for, and an often ridiculously light-hearted younger sister to worry about. No. Angelina Hunter had no time for the things most young women her age enjoyed.

And yet, Angelina had not always been so hardened. There had been a time when she boasted a fun, flirtatious nature even more delightful than her sister Becca's—a time when her imagination soared with adventurous, romantic dreams. But that all ended years before at the hand of one man. Her heart turned to stone…safely becoming void of any emotion save impatience and indifference.

Until the day her dreams returned, the day the very maker of her broken heart rode back into her life. As the dust settled from the cattle drive which brought him back, would Angelina's heart be softened? Would she learn to hope again? Would her long-lost dreams become a blessed reality?

Kiss in the Dark
Contemporary Romance

"Boston," he mumbled.

"I mean…Logan…he's like the man of my dreams! Why would I blow it? What if…" Boston continued to babble.

"Boston," he said. The commanding sound of his voice caused Boston to cease in her prattling and look to him.

"What?" she asked, somewhat grateful he'd interrupted her panic attack.

He frowned and shook his head.

"Shut up," he said. "You're all worked up about

nothing." He reached out, slipping one hand beneath her hair to the back of her neck.

Boston was so startled by his touch, she couldn't speak—she could only stare up into his mesmerizing green eyes. His hand was strong and warm, powerful and reassuring.

"If it freaks you out so much…just kiss in the dark," he said.

Boston watched as Vance put the heel of his free hand to the light switch. In an instant the room went black.

Kissing Cousins
Contemporary Romance

Poppy Amore loved her job waitressing at Good Ol' Days Family Restaurant. No one could ask for a better working environment. After all, her best friend Whitney worked there, and her boss, restaurant owner Mr. Dexter, was a kind, understanding, grandfatherly sort of man. Furthermore, the job allowed Poppy to linger in the company of Mr. Dexter's grandson Swaggart Moretti—the handsome and charismatic head cook at Good Ol' Days.

Secretly, Swaggart was far more to Poppy than just a man who was easy to look at. In truth, she had harbored a secret crush on him for years—since her freshman year in high school, in fact. And although the memory of her feelings—even the lingering truth of them—haunted Poppy the way a veiled, unrequited love always haunts a heart, she had learned to simply find joy in possessing a hidden, anonymous delight in merely being associated with Swaggart. Still, Poppy had begun to wonder if her heart would ever let go of Swaggart Moretti—if any other man in the world could ever turn her head.

When the dazzling, uber-fashionable Mark Lawson appeared one night at Good Ol' Days, however, Poppy began to believe that perhaps her attention and her heart would be distracted from Swaggart at last. Mark Lawson was every girl's fantasy—tall, uniquely handsome, financially well-off, and as charming as any prince ever to appear in fairy tales. He was kind, considerate, and, Poppy would find, a true, old-fashioned champion. Thus, Poppy Amore willingly allowed her heart and mind to follow Mark Lawson—to attempt to abandon the past and an unrequited love and begin to move on.

But all the world knows that real love is not so easily put off, and Poppy began to wonder if even a man so wonderful as Mark Lawson could truly drive Swaggart Moretti from her heart. Would Poppy Amore miss her one chance at happiness, all for the sake of an unfulfilled adolescent's dream?

Love Me
Contemporary Romance

Jacey Whittaker couldn't remember a time when she hadn't loved Scott Pendleton—the boy next door. She couldn't remember a time when Scott hadn't been in her life—in her heart. Yet Scott was every other girl's dream too. How could Jacey possibly hope to win such a prize—the attention, the affections, the very heart of such a sought-after young man? Yet win him she did! He became the bliss of her youthful heart—at least for a time.

Still, some dreams live fulfilled—and some are lost. Loss changes the very soul of a being. Jacey wondered if her soul would ever rebound. Certainly, she went on—lived a happy life—if not so full and perfectly happy a life as she once lived. Yet she feared she would never recover—never get over Scott Pendleton—her first love.

Until the day a man walked into her apartment—into her apartment and into her heart. Would this man be the one to heal her broken heart? Would this man be her one true love?

Saphyre Snow
Historical Romance

Descended of a legendary line of strength and beauty, Saphyre Snow had once known happiness as princess of the Kingdom of Graces. Once a valiant king had ruled in wisdom—once a loving mother had spoken soft words of truth to her daughter. Yet a strange madness had poisoned great minds—a strange fever inviting Lord Death to linger. Soon it was even Lord Death sought to claim Saphyre Snow for his own—and all Saphyre loved seemed lost.

Thus, Saphyre fled—forced to leave all familiars for necessity of preserving her life. Alone, and without provision, Saphyre knew Lord Death might yet claim her—for how could a princess hope to best the Reaper himself?

Still, fate often provides rescue by extraordinary venues, and Saphyre was not delivered into the hands of Death—but into the hands of those hiding dark secrets in the depths of bruised and bloodied souls. Saphyre knew a measure of hope and asylum in the company of these battered vagabonds. Even she knew love—a secreted love—a forbidden love. Yet it was love itself—even held secret—that would again summon Lord Death to hunt the princess, Saphyre Snow.

Shackles of Honor
Historical Romance

Cassidy Shea's life was nothing if not serene. Loving parents and a doting brother provided happiness and innocent hope in dreaming as life's experience. Yes, life was blissful at her beloved home of Terrill.

Still, for all its beauty and tranquility…ever there was something intangible and evasive lurking in the shadows. And though Cassidy wasted little worry on it…still she sensed its existence, looming as a menacing fate bent on ruin.

And when one day a dark stranger appeared, Cassidy could no longer ignore the ominous whispers of the secrets surrounding her. Mason Carlisle, an angry, unpredictable man materialized…and seemingly with Cassidy's black fate at his heels.

Instantly Cassidy found herself thrust into a world

completely unknown to her, wandering in a labyrinth of mystery and concealments. Serenity was vanquished… and with it, her dreams.

Or were all the secrets so guardedly kept from Cassidy…were they indeed the cloth, the very flax from which her dreams were spun? From which eternal bliss would be woven?

Sudden Storms
Historical Romance

Rivers Brighton was a wanderer—having nothing and belonging to no one. Still, by chance, Rivers found herself harboring for a time beneath the roof of the kind-hearted Jolee Gray and her remarkably attractive yet ever-grumbling brother, Paxton. Jolee had taken Rivers in, and Rivers had stayed.

Helplessly drawn to Paxton's alluring presence and unable to escape his astonishing hold over her, however, Rivers knew she was in danger of enduring great heartbreak and pain. Paxton appeared to find Rivers no more interesting than a brief cloudburst. Yet the man's spirit seemed to tether some great and devastating storm—a powerful tempest bridled within, waiting for the moment when it could rage full and free, perhaps destroying everything and everyone in its wake—particularly Rivers.

Could Rivers capture Paxton's attention long enough to make his heart her own? Or would the storm brewing within him destroy her hopes and dreams of belonging to the only man she had ever loved?

Sweet Cherry Ray
Historical Romance

Cherry glanced at her pa, who frowned and slightly shook his head. Still, she couldn't help herself, and she leaned over and looked down the road.

She could see the rider and his horse—a large buckskin stallion. As he rode nearer, she studied his white shirt, black flat-brimmed hat, and double-breasted vest. Ever nearer he rode, and she fancied his pants were almost the same color as his horse, with silver buttons running down the outer leg. Cherry had seen a similar manner of dress before—on the Mexican vaqueros that often worked for her pa in the fall.

"Cherry," her pa scolded in a whisper as the stranger neared them.

She straightened and blushed, embarrassed by being as impolite in her staring as the other town folk were in theirs. It seemed everyone had stopped whatever they had been doing to walk out to the street and watch the stranger ride in.

No one spoke—the only sound was that of the breeze, a falcon's cry overhead and the rhythm of the rider's horse as it slowed to a trot.

Take a Walk with Me
Contemporary Romance

"Grandma?" Cozy called as she closed the front door behind her. She inhaled a deep breath—bathing in the warm, inviting scent of banana nut bread baking in the oven. "Grandma? Are you in here?"

"Cozy!" her grandma called in a loud whisper. "I'm in the kitchen. Hurry!"

Cozy frowned—her heart leapt as worry consumed her for a moment. Yet, as she hurried to the kitchen to find her grandma kneeling at the window that faced the new neighbors yard, and peering out with a pair of binoculars, she exhaled a sigh of relief.

"Grandma! You're still spying on him?" she giggled.

"Get down! They'll see us! Get down!" Dottie ordered in a whisper, waving one hand in a gesture that Cozy should duck.

Giggling with amusement at her grandma's latest antics, Cozy dropped to her hands and knees and crawled toward the window.

"Who'll see us?" she asked.

"Here," Dottie whispered, pausing only long enough to reach for a second set of binoculars sitting on the nearby counter. "These are for you." She smiled at Cozy—winked as a grin of mischief spread over her face. "And now…may I present the entertainment for this evening…Mr. Buckly hunk of burning love Bryant…and company."

Romantic Vignettes—The Anthology of Premiere Novellas
Historical Romance
Includes Three Novellas:
The Unobtainable One

Annette Jordan had accepted the unavoidable reality that she must toil as a governess to provide for herself. Thankfully, her charge was a joy—a vision of youthful beauty, owning a spirit of delight.

But it was Annette's employer, Lord Gareth Barrett, who proved to be the trial—for she soon found herself living in the all-too-cliché governess's dream of having fallen desperately in love with the man who provided her wages.

The child loved her—but could she endure watching hopelessly as the beautiful woman from a neighboring property won Lord Barrett's affections?

The General's Ambition

Seemingly overnight, Renee Millings found herself orphaned and married to the indescribably handsome, but ever frowning, Roque Montan. His father, The General, was obsessively determined that his lineage would continue posthaste—with or without consent of his son's new bride.

But when Roque reveals the existence of a sworn oath that will obstruct his father's ambition, will the villainous General conspire to ensure the future of his coveted progeny to be born by Renee himself? Will Renee find the only means of escape from the odious General to be that of his late wife—death? Or will the son find no tolerance for his father's diabolic plotting concerning the woman Roque legally terms his wife?

Indebted Deliverance

Chalyce LaSalle had been grateful to the handsome recluse, Race Trevelian, when he had delivered her from certain tragedy one frigid winter day. He was addictively attractive, powerful, and intriguing—and there was something else about him—an air of secreted internal torture. Yet, as the brutal character of her emancipator began to manifest, Chalyce commenced in wondering whether the fate she now faced would be any less insufferable than the one from which he had delivered her.

Still, his very essence beckoned hers. She was drawn to him and her soul whispered that his mind needed deliverance as desperately as she had needed rescue that cold winter's noon.

The Fragrance of Her Name
Historical Romance

Love—the miraculous, eternal bond that binds two souls together. Lauryn Kennsington knew the depth of it. Since the day of her eighth birthday, she had lived the power of true love—witnessed it with her own heart. She had talked with it—learned not even time or death can vanquish it. The Captain taught her these truths—and she loved him all the more for it.

Yet now—as a grown woman—Lauryn's dear Captain's torment became her own. After ten years, Lauryn had not been able to help him find peace—the peace his lonely spirit so desperately needed—the peace he'd sought every moment since his death over fifty years before.

Still, what of her own peace? The time had come. Lauryn's heart longed to do the unthinkable—selfishly abandon her Captain for another—a mortal man who had stolen her heart—become her only desire.

Would Lauryn be able to put tormented spirits to rest and still be true to her own soul? Or, would she have to make a choice—a choice forcing her to sacrifice one true love for another?

The Heavenly Surrender
Historical Romance

Genieva Bankmans had willfully agreed to the arrangement. She had given her word, and she would not dishonor it. But when she saw, for the first time, the man whose advertisement she had answered… she was desperately intimidated. The handsome and commanding Brevan McLean was not what she had expected. He was not the sort of man she had reconciled herself to marrying.

This man, this stranger whose name Genieva now bore, was strong-willed, quick-tempered, and expectant of much from his new wife. Brevan McLean did not deny he had married her for very practical reasons only. He merely wanted any woman whose hard work would provide him assistance with the brutal demands of farm life.

But Genieva would learn there were far darker things, grave secrets held unspoken by Brevan McLean concerning his family and his land. Genieva Bankmans McLean was to find herself in the midst of treachery, violence, and villainy with her estranged husband deeply entangled in it.

The Highwayman of Tanglewood
Historical Romance

A chambermaid in the house of Tremeshton, Faris Shayhan well knew torment, despair, and trepidation. To Faris it seemed the future stretched long and desolate before her—bleak and as dark as a lonesome midnight path. Still, the moon oft casts hopeful luminosity to light one's way. So it was that Lady Maranda Rockrimmon cast hope upon Faris—set Faris upon a different path—a path of happiness, serenity, and love.

Thus, Faris abandoned the tainted air of Tremeshton in favor of the amethyst sunsets of Loch Loland Castle and her new mistress, Lady Rockrimmon. Further, it was on the very night of her emancipation that Faris first met the man of her dreams—the man of every woman's dreams—the rogue Highwayman of Tanglewood.

Dressed in black and astride his mighty steed, the brave, heroic, and dashing rogue Highwayman of Tanglewood stole Faris's heart as easily as he stole her kiss. Yet the Highwayman of Tanglewood was encircled in mystery—mystery as thick and as secretive as time itself. Could Faris truly own the heart of a man so entirely enveloped in twilight shadows and dangerous secrets?

The Light of the Lovers' Moon
Historical Romance

Violet Fynne was haunted—haunted by memory. It had been nearly ten years since her father had moved the family from the tiny town of Rattler Rock to the city of Albany, New York. Yet the pain and guilt in Violet's heart were as fresh and as haunting as ever they had been.

It was true Violet had been only a child when her family moved. Still—though she had been unwillingly pulled away from Rattler Rock—pulled away from him she held most dear—her heart had never left—and her mind had never forgotten the promise she had made—a promise to a boy—to a boy she had loved—a boy she had vowed to return to.

Yet the world changes—and people move beyond pain and regret. Thus, when Violet Fynne returned to Rattler Rock, it was to find that death had touched those she had known before—that the world had indeed changed—that unfamiliar faces now intruded on beloved memories.

Had she returned too late? Had Violet Fynne lost her chance for peace—and happiness? Would she be forever haunted by the memory of the boy she had loved nearly ten years before?

The Pirate Ruse

Historical Romance

Abducted! Forcibly taken from her home in New Orleans, Cristabel Albay found herself a prisoner aboard an enemy ship—and soon thereafter, transferred into the vile hands of blood-thirsty pirates! War waged between the newly liberated United States and King George. Still, Cristabel would soon discover that British sailors were the very least of her worries—for the pirate captain, Bully Booth, owned no loyalty—no sympathy for those he captured.

Yet hope was not entirely lost—for where there was found one crew of pirates—there was ever found another. Though Cristabel Albay would never have dreamed that she may find fortune in being captured by one pirate captain only to be taken by another—she did! Bully Booth took no man alive—let no woman live long. But the pirate Navarrone was known for his clemency. Thus, Cristabel's hope in knowing her life's continuance was restored.

Nonetheless, as Cristabel's heart began to yearn for the affections of her handsome, beguiling captor—she wondered if Captain Navarrone had only saved her life to execute her poor heart!

The Prairie Prince
Historical Romance

For Katie Matthews, life held no promise of true happiness. Life on the prairie was filled with hard labor, a brutal father, and the knowledge she would need to marry a man incapable of truly loving a woman. Men didn't have time to dote on women—so Katie's father told her. To Katie, it seemed life would forever remain mundane and disappointing—until the day Stover Steele bought her father's south acreage.

Handsome, rugged, and fiercely protective of four orphaned sisters, Stover Steele seemed to have stepped from the pages of some romantic novel. Yet his heroic character and alluring charm only served to remind Katie of what she would never have—true love and happiness the likes found only in fairytales. Furthermore, evil seemed to lurk in the shadows, threatening Katie's brightness, hope, and even her life!

Would Katie Matthews fall prey to disappointment, heartache, and harm? Or could she win the attentions of the handsome Stover Steele long enough to be rescued?

The Rogue Knight
Historical Romance

An aristocratic birthright and the luxurious comforts of profound wealth did nothing to comfort Fontaine Pratina following the death of her beloved parents. After two years in the guardianship of her mother's arrogant and selfish sister, Carileena Wetherton, Fontaine's only moments of joy and peace were found in the company of the loyal servants of Pratina Manor. Only in the kitchens and servants' quarters of her grand domicile did Fontaine find friendship, laughter, and affection.

Always, the life of a wealthy orphan destined to inherit loomed before her—a dark cloud of hopeless, shallow, snobbish people…a life of aristocracy, void of simple joys—and of love. Still, it was her lot—her birthright, and she saw no way of escaping it.

One brutal, cold winter's night a battered stranger appeared at the kitchen servants' entrance, however, seeking shelter and help. He gave only his first name, Knight…and suddenly, Fontaine found herself experiencing fleeting moments of joy in life. For

Knight was handsome, powerful...the very stuff of the legends of days of old. Though a servant's class was his, he was proud and strong, and even his name seemed to portray his persona absolutely. He distracted Fontaine from her dull, hopeless existence.

Yet there were devilish secrets—strategies cached by her greedy aunt, and not even the handsome and powerful Knight could save her from them. Or could he? And if he did—would the truth force Fontaine to forfeit her Knight, her heart's desire...the man she loved—in order to survive?

The Tide of the Mermaid Tears
Historical Romance

Ember Taffee had always lived with her mother and sister in the little cottage by the sea. Her father had once lived there too, but the deep had claimed his life long ago. Still, her existence was a happy one, and Ember found joy, imagination, and respite in the sea and the trinkets it would leave for her on the sand.

Each morning Ember would wander the shore searching for treasures left by the tides. Though she cherished each pretty shell she found, her favorite gifts from Neptune were the rare mermaid tears—bits of tinted glass worn smooth and lovely by the ocean. To Ember, in all the world there were no jewels lovelier than mermaid tears.

Yet one morning, Ember was to discover that Neptune would present her with a gift more rare than any other—something she would value far more than the shells and sea glass she collected. One morning Ember Taffee would find a living, breathing man washed up on the sand—a man who would own claim to her heart as full as Neptune himself owned claim to the seas.

The Time of Aspen Falls
Contemporary Romance

Aspen Falls was happy. Her life was good. Blessed with a wonderful family and a loyal best friend—Aspen did know a measure of contentment.

Still, to Aspen it seemed something was missing—something hovering just beyond her reach—something entirely satisfying that would ensure her happiness. Yet, she couldn't consciously determine what the "something" was. And so, Aspen sailed through life—not quite perfectly content perhaps—but grateful for her measure of contentment.

Grateful, that is, until he appeared—the man in the park—the stranger who jogged passed the bench where Aspen sat during her lunch break each day. As handsome as a dream, and twice as alluring, the man epitomized the absolute stereotypical "real man"—and Aspen's measure of contentment vanished!

Would Aspen Falls reclaim the comfortable contentment she once knew? Or would the handsome real-man-stranger linger in her mind like a sweet, tricky venom—poisoning all hope of Aspen's ever finding true happiness with any other man?

The Touch of Sage
Historical Romance

After the death of her parents, Sage Willows had lovingly nurtured her younger sisters through childhood, seeing each one married and never resenting not finding herself a good man to settle down with. Yet, regret is different than resentment.

Still, Sage found as much joy as a lonely young woman could find, as proprietress of Willows's Boarding House—finding some fulfillment in the companionship of the four beloved widow women boarding with her. But when the devilishly handsome Rebel Lee Mitchell appeared on the boarding house step, Sage's contentment was lost forever.

Dark, mysterious and secretly wounded, Reb Mitchell instantly captured Sage's lonely heart. But the attractive cowboy, admired and coveted by every young unmarried female in his path, seemed unobtainable to Sage Willows. How could a weathered, boarding house proprietress resigned to spinsterhood ever hope to capture the attention of such a man? And without him, would Sage Willows simply sink deeper into bleak loneliness—tormented by the knowledge that the man of every woman's dreams could never be hers?

The Trove of The Passion Room
Contemporary Romance

Sharlamagne Dickens cherished her family, was intrigued by the past, adored antiques, and enjoyed working at the antique store owned by her parents.

Her life, like most, had been touched by tragedy and loss, yet she was happy. Though her life was not void of romance, it was void of a certain emotional passion. Still, she was young and assumed that one day some man might manage to sweep her off her feet. Sharlamagne did not expect to be entirely bowled over, however. And the day she first set eyes on Maxim Tanner, she was!

Elisaveta Tanner's grandson, Maxim, was the dreamiest, most attractive archetypal male Sharlamagne and her sister, Gwen, had ever seen! Tall, dark, and illegally handsome, Maxim Tanner possessed not only fabulous looks, money, and the sweetest grandmother in the world but also a fair amount of local fame. He was gorgeous, clever, and pathetically out of reach for any average girl.

And so Sharlamagne went about her life happy and satisfied—for she had no idea what sort of emotional intensity the right man could inflame in her. She had no conception of how an age-old mystery and one man could converge to unleash a passion so powerful that it would be either the greatest gift she had ever known— or her final undoing.

The Visions of Ransom Lake
Historical Romance

Youthful beauty, naïve innocence, a romantic imagination thirsting for adventure…an apt description of Vaden Valmont, who would soon find the adventure and mystery she had always longed to experience…in the form of a man.

A somber recluse, Ransom Lake descended from his solitary concealment in the mountains, wholly uninterested in people and their trivial affairs. And somehow, young Vaden managed to be ever in his way...either by accident or because of her own unique ability to stumble into a quandary.

Yet the enigmatic Ransom Lake would involuntarily become Vaden's unwitting tutor. Through him, she would experience joy and passion the like even Vaden had never imagined. Yes, Vaden Valmont stepped innocently, yet irrevocably, into love with the secretive, seemingly callous man.

But there were other life's lessons Ransom Lake would inadvertently bring to her as well. The darker side of life—despair, guilt, heartache. Would Ransom Lake be the means of Vaden's dreams come true? Or the cause of her complete desolation?

The Whispered Kiss
Historical Romance

With the sea at its side, the beautiful township of Bostchelan was home to many—including the lovely Coquette de Bellamont, her three sisters, and beloved father. In Bostchelan, Coquette knew happiness and as much contentment as a young woman whose heart had been broken years before could know. Thus, Coquette dwelt in gladness until the day her father returned from his travels with an astonishing tale to tell.

Antoine de Bellamont returned from his travels by way of Roanan bearing a tale of such great adventure to hardly be believed. Further, at the center of Antoine's story loomed a man—the dark Lord of Roanan. Known for his cruel nature, heartlessness, and tendency to violence, the Lord of Roanan had accused Antoine de Bellamont of wrongdoing and demanded recompense. Antoine had promised recompense would be paid—with the hand of his youngest daughter in marriage.

Thus, Coquette found herself lost—thrust onto a dark journey of her own. This journey would find her carried away to Roanan Manor—delivered into the hands of the dark and mysterious Lord of Roanan who dominated it.

The Windswept Flame
Historical Romance

Broken—irreparably broken. The violent deaths of her father and the young man she'd been engaged to marry had irrevocably broken Cedar Dale's heart. Her mother's heart had been broken as well—shattered by the loss of her own true love. Thus, pain and anguish—fear and despair—found Cedar Dale and her mother, Flora, returned to the small western town where life had once been happy and filled with hope. Perhaps there Cedar and her mother would find some resemblance of truly living life—instead of merely existing. And then, a chance meeting with a dream from her past caused a flicker of wonder to ignite in her bosom.

As a child, Cedar Dale had adored the handsome rancher's son, Tom Evans. And when chance brought her face-to-face with the object of her childhood fascination once more, Cedar Dale began to believe that perhaps her fragmented heart could be healed.

Yet could Cedar truly hope to win the regard of such a man above men as was Tom Evans? A man kept occupied with hard work and ambition—a man so desperately sought after by seemingly every woman?

To Echo the Past
Historical Romance

As her family abandoned the excitement of the city for the uneventful lifestyle of a small, western town, Brynn Clarkston's worst fears were realized. Stripped of her heart's hopes and dreams, Brynn knew true loneliness.

Until an ordinary day revealed a heavenly oasis in the desert…Michael McCall. Handsome and irresistibly charming, Michael McCall (the son of legendary horse breeder Jackson McCall) seemed to offer wild distraction and sincere friendship to Brynn. But could Brynn be content with mere friendship when her dreams of Michael involved so much more?

Weathered Too Young
Historical Romance

Lark Lawrence was alone. In all the world there was no one who cared for her. Still, there were worse things than independence—and Lark had grown quite capable of providing for herself. Nevertheless, as winter loomed, she suddenly found herself with no means by which to afford food and shelter—destitute.

Yet Tom Evans was a kind and compassionate man. When Lark Lawrence appeared on his porch, without pause he hired her to keep house and cook for himself and his cantankerous elder brother, Slater. And although Tom had befriend Lark first, it would be Slater Evans—handsome, brooding, and twelve years Lark's senior—who would unknowingly abduct her heart.

Still, Lark's true age (which she concealed at first meeting the Evans brothers) was not the only truth she had kept from Slater and Tom Evans. Darker secrets lay imprisoned deep within her heart—and her past. However, it is that secrets are made to be found out— and Lark's secrets revealed would soon couple with the arrival of a woman from Slater's past to forever shatter her dreams of winning his love—or so it seemed. Would truth and passion mingle to capture Lark the love she'd never dared to hope for?

PURCHASED AT PUBLIC SALE
SURPLUS MATERIALS

CPSIA information can be obtained at www.ICGtesting.com
Printed in the USA
LVOW011609311011

252875LV00014B/19/P

9 780983 807469